KILLING KARMA Copyright © 2022 by Michael Poeltl.

For information, contact Michael Poeltl at
mikepoeltl@hotmail.com

Cover design by *MP*

FIRST EDITION
ISBN 978-0-9952885-3-9

Detective fiction 2. Crime fiction 3. Paranormal fiction
4. American literature 5. Suspense 6. Thriller

Michael Poeltl

No Karmic debt ever goes unpaid.

Michael Poeltl

CHAPTERS

Michael Poeltl

The Karma Killer

You reap what you sow.

Newton's law of universal gravitation states that every particle attracts every other particle in the universe with a force that is directly proportional to the product of their masses. Karma acts similarly in that your experiences are directly proportional to the experiences you put out in the world. Karma transcends the present. It follows you through lifetimes. It is a natural law, and like gravity, it doesn't cease to exist if you don't believe in it. Gravity keeps your feet on the ground, the moon in orbit, and the planets moving around the sun. Karma shares this omnipotent quality. Karma keeps you honest. It carries out cause and effect in its own time, and what you reap, you will sow.

We live in the present, but it is a difficult place for many. Karmic debts are continuously being disbursed in many forms. Some will experience poverty while others have great wealth. Some will be sickly, while others can't seem to catch a cold. Some will offer kindness to those who'd showed them a similar kindness in another life. Some will die at the hands of those they'd wronged in a shared past.

Karma goes both ways. It is a perfect accounting system that none can avoid, and like gravity, it is a constant. It works through people unconsciously participating in its greater plan.

No karmic debt ever goes unpaid, but sometimes it needs a nudge.

Karma has a champion.

Chapter 1

Having never seen action, Peter thought he'd avoid the punishing effects of post-traumatic stress disorder, but in hindsight, as a peacekeeper in a foreign land, that reality shouldn't have been far from his mind.

Stationed in Kandahar province in August of 2021, he and his fellow soldiers were ordered to fall back to the airport where embassy and military personnel were being flown out of Afghanistan. The threat Peter was asked to secure was not the encroaching Taliban forces but the citizens who, in fits of despair over their newly won government, begged to be put on planes and evacuated along with the fleeing military personnel and ambassadors who had helped win back their country.

The scene was one of continuous chaos - day and night for many days. Peter stood watch where only chain-link fencing kept people at bay after bombs crumbled the tall cement walls before. Pleas from the growing crowds to let their children through tugged at his conscience. Hateful cries against the escaping forces leaving them to their fates were soul-crushing. Their voices cracked with anguish under the weight of another Taliban rule. It reminded Peter of the third panel in Hieronymus Bosch's The Garden of Earthly Delights. Chaos. *Hell.* And he had perpetrated that hell for those people: Pointing rifles and shouting for them to step back. All he wanted to do was help them, but he was a soldier put in a position he hadn't imagined. He relied on his training to steady his nerves. In the moment, it worked. It's what happens after that isn't easily discussed.

Often children were pushed to the front of the terminals to appeal to the soldier's morality. Peter had befriended three of them with what little of the native Pashto he spoke. He had given them candies and water during the calmer moments. When, on that fateful day, a suicide bomber entered the airport, Peter watched those three children become engulfed in the explosion. Rifles fired by frightened soldiers threw hot lead at the crowd who were caught up in a focused charge through the terminal and onto the tarmac in a desperate attempt to escape the chaos and board the military aircraft already moving down the runway. Peter, too, fired on the unfortunate masses – his training overriding his better judgment. His vision had narrowed, and the blood in his ears *thumped, thumped, thumped* against his temples as he instinctively backed away from the stampeding horde. The smell of the detonated explosive and the charred flesh of the innocents permeated his senses. He felt sick to his stomach. It was at that moment he experienced real anxiety for the first time.

His magazine emptied into the air, trying to alter the hoard's trajectory, but the people were not deterred. They fell over the dead, and they fell over the living. They clambered for purchase over one another. The screaming filled Peter's awareness, distorting everyone and everything. He watched helplessly as hundreds stormed the airfield and even leaped onto the landing gear. The aircraft did not falter. A line of bodies on the tarmac followed where the great wheels had run them over. Blood ran like a river collecting in a reservoir where the edge of the runway dipped slightly to the right. The scene was grotesque, and again Peter thought of Bosch's absurd painting.

But that was last year, and Peter vows to get better this year. Several months out of the service, he reconnected with his past love of reading and became store manager of a small but popular bookstore in the Cornerstone Village district of Detroit. He'd chosen a new city a thousand miles removed from his hometown to separate himself from anything that might trigger his PTSD. Peter is something of a recluse. He feels he's lost his knack for developing interpersonal relationships and has trouble trusting people. Besides, who would want to be with a damaged Vet like him? Peter is content, interacting with enough people daily that he is comfortable being alone in the evenings when he is not at the bookstore. He enjoys the occasional conversation featuring reading lists and favorite books but tries not to go beyond those topics. He never speaks of his time overseas unless it is at one of his veteran-sanctioned counseling sessions. At night Peter finds himself back in Kandahar, firing his rifle at civilians. Sometimes he is the civilian being fired upon. Sometimes he is the birdman devouring a human leg in the third panel of Bosch's The Garden of Earthly Delights. PTSD haunts his sleep. It shadows him every second of the day, emerging in his most vulnerable moments. The counseling helps, but it doesn't seem like enough. Maybe nothing ever will be.

After a troubling session with Group, Peter makes his way home, where he rents a two-bedroom apartment above the bookstore he manages. It is an excellent pairing for Peter. He often enters the store during his sleepless nights to read some obscure tome until morning. The potent smell of so many books brings him peace and presence, while reading gives his mind something to focus on. On June 7th, 2022, a young woman enters the bookstore. She seems out of place in Cornerstone Village, but Peter welcomes her patronage. She is lovely, whereas Cornerstone Village is, well, not.

"Hi," the woman looks in her mid-to-late-twenties, Peter guesses. Maybe two years his junior. Her stoic expression does nothing to complement her tiny features. The high-set, messy bun holding her dirty-blonde hair in place adds a sense of resolve flattering her conservative outfit. "I'm Clare," she announces. "Hello, Clare," Peter replies with his customary smile that raises the right side of his face. "I'm Peter."

"I'm here for the book," she continues, seemingly uninterested in his name. She reads the confusion on his face. "I'm Clare? Clare Hastings?" Her eyes locked on Peter's, shifting left to his computer screen as if insisting he finds her there.

Peter thinks her pretty in that mousey, bookish way. He concedes the nonverbal signal, nodding and stepping to his right to pull up the order screen. "Miss Hastings, yes, your book is in," Peter bends down to find the package under the counter. The book is called *The Many Lives of Mr. Jones.* "A curious title," he says.

"It's about his past lives." She says curtly, taking the book from Peter. "Is there a receipt?" Peter looks at the screen again and asks, "would you like that printed or emailed?"

"Printed, please." Peter does so and hands the receipt to Miss Hastings. "Do you have any other books like this on the shelves?" She glances to her left, where four tall, dark wooden racks create five eight-foot aisles filled with books.

"About past lives? No, I don't think we do." Peter has a relationship with all the books in the shop. If he hasn't already read them, he knows what he's ordered. "I've never read a book on that topic. It sounds fascinating."

"You should look it up. There are lots of books on people coming back." The woman stands stock still with the new book flat against her small chest, arms crossing over it.

"From the dead?" Peter teases, finding it strangely easy to talk to this woman.

"From the – no, no," Peter catches the whisper of a smile play across her painted lips. "Well, in a way, I guess that's an apt description. But not like a *zombie*. You die and then come back as another life."

"Like the soul reanimating and so on."

"Right, exactly like that. I've been mesmerized by the genre for years." Peter hadn't expected Clare to open up like this but is enjoying the sound of her voice, husky but feminine. "So much so that I've participated in past life regression." She notes Peter's confusion and continues. "It's where you're hypnotized and asked to relive some of your past lives. It's utterly intriguing. The regressionist even records your session so you can listen to it again and again."

"Hypnotized? That's – is it easy to be hypnotized?"

"She knew I would be easy to put under on account of my imaginative nature. A creative mind is an accepting one." Clare seems surprised at herself for running on like this, and Peter thinks he experiences a genuine smile from her. "It's used as therapy on some people. They say the lives you live when regressing assist in your present somehow. I haven't gone so far as to benefit from that angle, but it works from what I've researched. I suggest it to everyone I meet."

"Does that include me?" Peter asks playfully.

"Of course, we've only just met." Clare moves her hips and tilts her torso slightly in a mock curtsy. "Thank you for ordering the book. I'll certainly be back." She spins on her heels and moves toward the antique glass door.

"Would you give me the number of the, uh, regressionist you used?" The question forms before he can truly process it. "I think I can see myself trying that." Clare turns again, walks back to the counter, lays her book down, and removes a scrap piece of paper from her bag. Peter hands her a pen, and she jotted down an email. He notices her perfume's sweet yet subtle scent as she leans in.

"Send her a note. Her name is Theresa Clement. I'm sure she won't remember me, so it will do you no good to mention my name. It won't get you a discount or anything." She retrieves her book and studies Peter's expression, nods, and turns.

"Thanks?" Peter calls after her, and the bells over the door ring as Clare passes through the threshold. Peter's attention falls to the note. Clare's handwriting is pretty and neat. He types the address into his email client. The PTSD has become a nagging issue of late, and he feels at his wits' end with conventional therapy. Perhaps the road less traveled will offer results?

Chapter 2

The moment Theresa let her guard down and gave life a chance was the moment she knew things would start to get better. Trauma breeds purpose, and it was Theresa's traumatic discovery at her family home on Blackburn Steet that put her on a path she hadn't envisioned for herself. When regression therapy was offered as an alternative method to counseling, she felt a spark of recognition. It was inexplicable how the mere suggestion comforted her. She immediately took to the process and decided she would become a past life regressionist herself in a moment of uncharacteristic spontaneity. By 2013 she had completed a course in Lafayette, California. She had plenty of money to pursue whatever path she felt compelled to follow. The course modalities included Hypnotherapy, Reiki, Emotional Freedom Technique, and Bi-lateral Stimulation. These invoked balance, creativity, self-awareness, intuition, and grounding, which quickly accelerated her personal growth. The work and the therapy helped in understanding the guilt she harbored. But it would be a long road to recovery. The training also helped solidify her life path, and Theresa moved back to her parents' home to begin practicing her new career.

By 2018 she had established herself as the premiere regression therapist in her community. She had remodeled the 1960s bungalow she'd grown up in and created an office space from her old bedroom. The International Board for Regression Therapy assisted in guiding her on how she should proceed. Tasteful décor, including candles, salt lamps, oil diffusers, singing bowls, and crystals, gave the space a quality that set her and her clients at ease. A comfortable lounge and weighted blankets offered an additional sense of security during the sessions. It wasn't an easy road convincing people that reliving a past life could assist in bringing emotions and memories from the present to head, but the proof - as they say - is in the pudding.

Theresa found her stride, and the people came. Today she has a steady list of return clients and many one-offs. These come in the form of bachelorette and birthday parties as if she were offering little more than entertainment. But they also come in as serious queries. A small percentage of these become return clients, and this is how she maintains the business.

When Peter arrives for his appointment on June 9th, she reads him immediately. There is a deep well of sadness behind his eyes. *Is it guilt?* She knows that look all too well. There is something else, though. Something closer to the surface. She feels lonely in his presence. He is attractive enough, and just 28-years-old she's noted on the printed form in her hand. Theresa senses a connection to Peter that goes beyond his pain. She will have to meditate on this.

"Hello, Peter," she receives him with a short bow, "please take a seat." Peter bows awkwardly, and she smiles serenely at this. He thanks her and sits on the plush fabric couch beside the door, hands folded on his lap. She notes his discomfort and smiles brightly at him, sitting in the high-backed chair opposite.

"I – uh, thank you for seeing me; I'm new to this." Peter offers nervously.

"Most are, Peter; you don't need to feel uncomfortable with me. I'm not reading your mind or anything," she laughs, and he allows himself a nervous chortle. "What brings you to see me today?"

"Well, I guess my PTSD. From the – uh, Afghanistan."

"Okay, and nothing has changed for you since you filled out the online form? It's the PTSD you want to address with therapy, then?" The question is more of a statement, and she notes the confirmation with a checkmark on the printout. "I can tell you I've performed several regression sessions for this very condition," Theresa explains, quietly acknowledging her struggle with PTSD. Though she will not share her experience with him, she certainly empathizes.

"That's reassuring," Peter admits. "It's been a real issue - getting back into a normal routine. A normal life."

"It's a brave thing to accept new therapies or any at all. You've made a decisive step just coming to this consultation." Theresa celebrates Peter's choice to encourage him further. "You mentioned on the form you've been in Group counseling and attended several one-on-one sessions with psychiatrists. You must have gained some powerful and necessary skills to cope?"

Peter nods yes. "It's been a long road, but I have some tools to get me past certain triggers. Still, it feels as if I'm constantly fighting back the memories. I wonder if I'm going through this for a reason. To overcome some deeper issues. Does that make sense?"

Theresa sits back and nods at Peter, maintaining eye contact. "That's very astute. In my practice, I bring your forgotten past to the forefront to assist in dealing with your present."

"My past lives," Peter says somewhat sarcastically. "I'm sorry, I didn't mean it like that. I'm still trying to get my head around it. I'm not a religious person."

"Then this may resonate with you all the more," she explains. "Regression into a past life is asking a lot of a person experiencing this life. The present is all about what we can see and smell and feel, you know? But in my experience, we've all been here before, and our consciousness has inhabited bodies and lived and learned. It's from past lessons that we can address your PTSD in this life."

"It's certainly a fascinating concept," Peter admits. Theresa notices how he wrings his hands, and she reaches across the coffee table, placing a hand atop his. The wringing stops, and Peter looks up at her. "A habit I developed over the last year." His hands release, and his palms slide over his thighs. Theresa slowly sinks back into her chair. "I've had other strange tics I've managed to overcome, but this one," he pauses, clearly embarrassed, "this one seems to have taken up residency. My hands are so smooth now," he laughs at himself, showing her his palms. "it's kind of ridiculous. I feel like I'm exfoliating myself to death."

"The wringing of hands is a practice of the guilty, Peter. You're not guilty of anything." Theresa uses this to draw out more information on the origins of his PTSD.

"Aren't I?" He looks up at her again and unconsciously returns to the activity. "I kept people from boarding those planes in Kandahar. The bomber and resulting stampede was a result of that."

"I remember seeing that in the news. I'm sorry you feel responsible, but if I recall, you were also protecting others as they boarded those planes to return home."

Peter's expression hardens. "Yes, but the carnage that followed, and for what? Why were we there at all? Spent billions of dollars and so many lives to replace the Taliban with the Taliban. Makes no sense."

"I appreciate what you're saying, Peter, and it's important that you are self-aware of the root cause of your PTSD in the present. It will make choosing the lives you'll face in regression that much easier." Theresa scribbles some notes and returns her attention to Peter. "I'd like to get started as soon as possible. Are you able to come tomorrow anytime between three and seven?"

Peter releases a shaky breath. "I'll be closing the shop at 5:30 tomorrow, so six would work."

"That gives us time then. I'll block off the seven o'clock, and we'll work until we're satisfied with your progress. You may want to clear your evening."

"Will it take that long?"

"I don't like to put a time limit on initial sessions. I want you to find your peace as the trance induction can take up to 45 minutes depending on the person, and then I can better assess timelines moving forward."

"I'm a little terrified over what we'll discover," he admits, studying his hands.

"Don't think of it like that. It's a healing process. Whatever we discover is designed to assist in overcoming your PTSD. It helps a person return to a trauma to understand the impact that trauma may be having on their current life or behaviors. Current issues may have their origins in a past life, and so in bringing them forth, we heal. It can be difficult, but I believe that hypnotic regression into your past lives is like tapping into an ethereal teacher, but that teacher is you. It's your spirit."

Peter lets out a sigh, "wow, you really believe in what you do."

"I do, and you'll believe it too." Theresa stands to encourage Peter, who also stands. "Tomorrow then. Six pm." He follows her to the front door, and she opens it for him. He nods and exits her parents' home.

Theresa considers the conversation and notices she has begun to wring her hands. She releases them immediately, straightens her skirt, and thinks, *we're all guilty of something.*

Chapter 3

It was a tough case that ended badly, Harlow recounts. It's the one that got away and has plagued his confidence with every new case he takes on. That was 11 years ago, but the self-doubt has never left him. Having made detective just months before the killings, he approached the scene with youthful ignorance. Sure, he had the training, but this would be his first lead investigation into a double murder. The reporters were chomping at the bit to sensationalize it and at his throat 24/7. His captain at the time had urged him to keep his focus on the investigation and not let anything slip as he fielded questions at the scene.

"Reporters can be ruthless and entitled, Harlow," he'd offered. "Give them nothing they can use to scare the perp into hiding. You've been briefed on this. Just the basic facts. Any evidence, no matter how impressive, cannot be released to the general public."

It was good advice, he remembered, but also a warning. *Don't fuck this up.* The crime was violent and bloody. The residence was in shambles as the perps had ransacked the house for whatever valuables presented themselves. It seemed a classic junkie hit at first sight. Disorganized. Rushed. Probably the murders weren't planned. The couple's lifeless bodies resulted from the murderous home invasion in 2011. Just a couple of meth-heads feeling the pull of their addictions trying front doors until one opened. In his experience, they'd push past any perceived obstacles to their next hit with reckless violence.

Signs of a struggle were everywhere. The broken glass dining table, the lamp, the skin recovered from under the female's fingernails, and the classic defense bruising on both victims' forearms. Eventually, they succumbed to the perp's beatings and hemorrhaged from head trauma not two feet apart on the carpeted dining room floor.

The ensuing investigation gave up one perp's DNA and the fingerprints of both. Neither turned up in the system, so Harlow had little to run with. As the middle-class neighborhood was canvased, others recalled their motion-sensor lights coming on. Some recounted sounds at their doors and windows that night, but no one had a security camera to identify the perps. It was a frustrating start to a brutal crime, and the newspapers were beginning to develop their own hypothesis. It was an embarrassment that stretched on for weeks.

It did end, however. Not with an arrest, but with another double murder. When the newly deceased were fingerprinted, Harlow realized his case was closed. Two tweekers were found in an alley in one of Detroit's less affluent neighborhoods. It was a curious scene. Both bludgeoned to death, needles dangling from their arms. Would he open an investigation on these two murders?

Who would care? The city was satisfied to know the murderers were dead. Was it a vigilante who sought out the Clement's murderers? That never went over well at the station. So, Harlow chalked it up as a failure with a satisfactory outcome.

His failure was felt strongest when he delivered the news to the couple's surviving teenager. She breathed a visible sigh of relief over the deaths of her parent's killers, but he felt compelled to ask her about her whereabouts the night before. She offered a curt response that checked out. She berated him for the insinuation and slammed the door in his face, but not before scolding him for the time it took to find those responsible and then having the audacity to accuse her. The victim's daughter was as disappointed in him as he had been in himself.

Still, he was credited as the lead investigator in a closed case. That never sat well with him, but he wouldn't contest it. He just acknowledged the honor and moved forward with his career, one that had flourished under the tutelage of his captain and the work he put into never allowing another case to end the way that one had.

Presently, Harlow is content Detroit has accepted him as one homicide after another is solved through diligent investigative work backed by years of experience. He is a well-decorated detective who has seen it all. At least, that was his assumption until the calling card of a potential serial killer surfaced.

Chapter 4

Peter takes a call from his mother at his apartment over the bookstore. She worries about him. She's always worried about him. She almost lost her mind when he joined the military to follow in his father's footsteps. His father is a mess these days. Peter is sure he'd suffered a similar condition, having served most of his life but was too proud to seek treatment. It wasn't done. His mother was the one who had urged Peter to find help for the trauma he'd experienced. To get help for his PTSD. She is a good mother.

"I'm fine, mom," is his practiced response. "I love the bookstore and am meeting all kinds of people through it." This is offered mainly to satisfy her need for tangible proof. Since he moved a thousand miles away from his family home, she can't just stop in and visit. Besides, she is caretaker to his father now that dementia has robbed him of his independence.

"I am beginning a new therapy tomorrow. Yes, it's going to help. No, I'm not lonely... yes, I'll be sure to do that. Thanks for calling mom. Love you. Remember me to dad. Bye."

He is lonely. But he's hesitant to build a friend base or date until he feels better about himself. The anxiety and sudden panic attacks are not something he can or is willing to explain to an unqualified stranger. For now, he is just going to do his job and concentrate on being better.

The following day Peter takes his coffee down the steps into the bookstore and turns on the lights. He's surprised to see a customer waiting at the door. It's a middle-aged man seemingly dressed for a formal occasion. Peter approaches the glass door and points at his watch. "We're not open for another half hour." He calls to the man.

"You have a book I need," the man shouts his reply, pointing at the display in the picture window. He looks frantic. It's a popular Chic-lit Peter had placed two days ago after receiving a shipment of twenty. This guy doesn't look the Rom-Com type, but Peter's seen stranger pairings with his books. "The thing is, it's a gift for a friend, and I can't get it from Amazon until next week. I'm seeing her tonight. Could I just pop in and pop out?"

The man's explanation offers resolution to Peter's question, and he doesn't see the harm in opening early. He unlocks the door and pulls it open for the older man. The bell rings overhead, and the man snatches up a copy and pays in cash. "Thank you so much. You're a lifesaver. It's her birthday, and this is her favorite author."

Peter nods and offers change for the purchase, but the man waves him off and is out the door in a flash.

Peter shrugs and turns his sign from *closed* to *open.* *Why not?* He saunters off to his counter and logs into the computer. An excellent start to the day, he thinks.

Not ten minutes later, another man, much older, enters with a small dog cradled in his arms. "I'm afraid I've walked her too far today," he explains, an expression of worry lining his already wrinkled face. Peter nods and smiles.

"How can I help you?"

"I hadn't expected to come here today." The elderly man admits, absently staring at Peter. "But that you're open, perhaps a book on dogs, I think. Just a story that involves a dog." The man looks kindly at the ball of white fluff in his arms and notices Peter smiling down at them. "She's fourteen, if you can believe it," the animated little man explains. "Still walks with me daily. Today though," he looks alarmingly around him, "we seem to have miscalculated our route."

Peter has never seen the man in his store before but feels a strange connection to him. Perhaps he's suffering the onset of Alzheimer's or a touch of dementia, like his father. He smells of sandalwood and sweat and looks lost but unwilling to admit it. "I've several books with dogs as the main character if that's what you mean, sir."

"Oh, that would be lovely," he rests a weathered, brown hand on the counter. "I like to read them to Lyla here."

Peter rounds the counter and collects three books that match the man's request from one of the shelves.

"We're not normally open quite yet, but this morning has been a busy one," Peter tells him, making conversation. The well-dressed gentleman looks as though he had attempted to shave but forgotten the right side of his face. He looks inquisitively at the books on the counter, picking each one up and reading the backs.

"And I'm rarely this far from home, so your being open has been a blessing for us both. I'll take all three, please."

"That will be forty-three, twenty-five, please." Peter rings up the books, and the older man pulls out his wallet. His arthritic hands struggle with a card, but he manages one and taps it, taking the bag of books. He looks around the shop a moment longer, and Peter again surfaces from behind his counter, opening the front door. "Would you like me to help you home, sir?"

The man nods emphatically and kisses Lyla's unkempt hair. "That would be very kind of you."

"I can lock up for now. It's no bother." Peter takes the man up the street to a traffic light, where they wait to cross.

"You seem a familiar face, son. Do we know each other?"

"I can't say that we do, sir. I'm Peter."

"I'm, uh, Mohamad." He offers his free hand, and Peter shakes it. It's icy. "You are good to help."

"It's okay; I'm happy to do it." And he is. Peter wants to help. It's what led him to enlist initially. He was not smart enough to become a medical doctor or psychiatrist, and reinforced by his father's stories about how his military career allowed him to serve humanity; he found the direction to do something worthwhile with his life.

The two men chat about the weather while navigating the ten blocks to Mohamad's apartment. There he thanks Peter again, and Peter rushes back to the bookstore.

"It's not like you to be late, Banks," Peter's boss stands at the door rooting through his satchel for the key. It's been over five weeks since Sanderson had shown up at the shop. Peter's been keeping count. "You do still live upstairs, do you not?"

"Sorry, Mr. Sanderson, I had an early customer who needed some assistance-"

"You're paid to sell books, not run errands for others," he snaps. "I have half a dozen hardcovers in my bag preying on my sciatica." Peter unlocks the door and holds it for Mr. Sanderson.

"Won't happen again," Peter promises. Likely it won't, but he'll do the same if it does.

"Place looks clean at least," Sanderson says in a huff, landing the books heavily on the counter. "These will go in the specialty case. Classics worth a mint. Catalog them and put them up on our website immediately. I'll fetch a pretty penny for these."

"Excellent," Peter tries to lighten the mood. Rocky starts with Sanderson never seem to right themselves.

He's a wet blanket - a killjoy in his early 60s with two ex-wives and a third who seems intent on leaving him. *Why would anyone marry three times?*

"I'm going to stick around a while today," Sanderson tells him, "Rather be in the books than in the doghouse again." He winks at Peter as if he can relate.

Peter doesn't like Mr. Sanderson, but he doesn't hate him either. They're very different people. He's cheap, and much of Peter's salary goes toward renting the apartment, but it's a situation that works for him for the moment.

Chapter 5

Theresa wonders what will come of Peter's session tonight. It's always an exciting trip to take with her clients when they make seemingly unconscious decisions to open the doors to past lives while in a trance. Though she appreciates that no choices while under the spell of hypnosis are unconscious. Every choice is made consciously through the spirit. It is the spirit she is witnessing while the body enters the trance.

After a two-hour session, she disinfects her lounge, where the client left teary-eyed and grateful for her lesson. It's a very personal experience, and Theresa feels honored to be allowed into another person's life – or lives – while they describe what they're experiencing. Afterward, she will sit with them, repeating the highlights, and offer counseling on how a life or lives can teach the client about their present trauma. It's enlightening for both. It's how she experiences life, she thinks.

As a relative recluse, Theresa knows she has not lived her own life to its fullest. She hasn't allowed herself to get close enough to a stranger to form a romantic relationship since she was 18. She has no children or even any family to speak of. Her mother's sister lives in Halifax, and her father didn't have siblings. After the funeral, of course, they vowed to stay in touch, but that lasted three years, and now it's the obligatory emails at Christmas and birthdays.

When she rallies the courage to go out, she has one friend who shares everything with her. Theresa met Nyra in high school. Nyra, the cheerleader, and Theresa, the wallflower. Still, for whatever reason, probably because their parents were old friends, Nyra took Theresa under her wing, getting her involved with the popular crowd and forcing her out of her shell. Theresa remembers that it was a lot of work and a lot of fun. She wouldn't have had half the experiences she had without Nyra in her life. Their friendship prepared her for college, where she briefly thrived on the social scene. Theresa and Nyra have a special bond where Theresa asks questions, and Nyra answers freely. Nyra knows Theresa's past and understands her need to live vicariously through her. She reports her good and bad decisions in raising her three children, marriage, vacations, and celebrations. Theresa knows Nyra would like to hear about her own experiences, but she has none to offer. None she feels she can. Client/therapist privilege keeps her from relating any of her practice, and she simply has nothing else. Still, one-sided conversations are hard on the other person. They must dredge up all their histories just to keep an evening going. Would Nyra eventually grow tired of her constant questions? Maybe. But people, Theresa has experienced, like to talk about themselves. Theresa would be sad to lose her for not participating in similar stories of her own. Perhaps she ought to be more adventurous. The deaths of her parent's made her meek. Sure, she traveled to go to school, but that was to get away from the house and its memories. While studying, she had her father's friend, a contractor, replace the carpet with laminate hardwood and manage a few minor upgrades to the house. When she returned from school, she asked him to build her a treatment room.

Though the experience was good for her, she felt the anxiety creep back upon returning home. Perhaps she should have just moved. But then, she didn't want to erase their memory. She loved her childhood home and felt grateful she could afford to keep it. She'd decided it was still a safe place regardless of what had happened. To say she was conflicted over the decision is putting it lightly. With ten years behind her, the renovation, and a career, Theresa no longer questions her motives.

She enters the kitchen and wishes she had had the wall removed separating the front dining room. Open concept is how people are building these days. Still, she never really spends any time in the dining room. It was made into a sitting room where she assesses potential clients. Ten to fifteen minutes at a time. It's enough.

Theresa warms up leftovers from the night before and sits at the kitchen counter to eat. She's lonely at times. It might be nice to have a partner. She's still young. She's not ugly, she concedes, but her nose is longer than most. Her eyes aren't too far apart or close together, and her lips aren't as thin as some. Her dark, black hair is long but not so thick as to require copious amounts of conditioner. It does tend to make her look paler than she is, though. She's a few pounds overweight which collects on her thighs, but she's not an unattractive person. She hates to judge herself and refuses to most days. She discourages judging others based on their appearance, catching herself when she does, rather judging them on their actions or inaction.

Back to that, Peter seems a good person caught up in the gravity of self-assessment. He was a soldier following orders. He gave his peers and those under his protection time to flee a country that had reverted to its former Taliban rule. She wonders what lives he might discover tonight to help him put his current life into perspective.

He's pretty handsome, she thinks. Tall, lean muscle under his fitted button-up, she imagines. His chestnut hair is cut short and falls neatly over his brown, piercing eyes. Ears tight against his head, a straight nose, and kissable lips. She gives her head a shake. She would never risk a client for a relationship and pushes the thought from her mind. He's come to her for help, and she will provide that for him, or at least open the doors that will assist in his recovery.

Theresa places her dishes in the sink and runs the tap. She hates to use the dishwasher for single meals and won't let them build up so she can use the appliance. No, like her father, she hand-washes everything. The act itself incites his memory. He was a good father, always with a kind word. He was an excellent husband who provided for his stay-at-home wife. Mom had held only one job before they'd met and married. They were always touching one another. Touch was their way of saying *I love you.* Theresa feels a warmth in her chest at the memories and pushes her glasses higher on her nose.

Why they were taken in such a violent, meaningless manner was a point of contention for her.

How good people fell to the desires of the wicked kept her awake in those early years. She better understands life's plan now. She sees the lives of others unfold on her chaise and how they play into their present. Life isn't so much a mystery to Theresa anymore as it is a muddied path to enlightenment.

She expects to achieve great things with Peter in the coming weeks as he volunteers his past lives in the hopes of realizing his purpose in this life. Or at least discover the reason for his misplaced guilt.

Chapter 6

Sanderson has been in Peter's personal space the whole day. He's hiding out. *His wife must be pissed about something.* He sits in the back office with his feet up on the small, cluttered desk. Peter notices a few file folders on the floor pushed off by the oaf's giant loafers. Sanderson is always dressed like he's going to a wedding. His sports jacket is flung over the back of the chair, and he's picking his nose. Literally. Peter shakes his head and wonders how he's found three wives to love him, however briefly.

Peter clears his throat at the office door. "I'm going to close now," he says, thrusting a thumb toward the door as if that would encourage the boss to leave.

"Hey? It's not 6." Sanderson's feet slide off the end of the desk, clearing more stationery to the floor. "Oh, damn it." He bends to pick up the pens, wheezing through the motion. "Don't we stay open until 6?"

"Not on Thursdays," Peter reminds him. "But if you want to stay, I'll leave the front open for you to lock up."

A heavy sigh from Sanderson irritates Peter. "Well, if I must, I must."

"*Really,* we close at 5:30 today," Peter pulls the keys from his pocket and removes the spare front door key. He sets it on the desk. "If you're going to leave the door unlocked, I'd position myself at the counter."

"You can't stay a little longer?"

"No, I have an appointment."

"Who sees anyone after 5?" Sanderson's tone puts Peter on edge. Though he can't afford to lose this job or his apartment, he can't miss his regression session.

"It's a personal matter," Peter offers. "I'm not comfortable discussing it."

Sanderson's interest is piqued. "Oh? A lady friend, maybe? The girls on the corner stay out all night." He laughs, thinking himself witty, referring to the hookers who've staked a claim to a corner a few blocks up.

"Not my speed," Peter replies. "You get home safe." He always takes the high road but wishes one day he'd be able to take the road less traveled and tell the fat fuck off. Peter leaves the office listening to the angry mumbling from the back of the store. Anxiety rumbles around in his chest, threatening to overwhelm him.

On the street, he shakes off the hostility the encounter left him with. *The whole day with that ass hat. I feel for his wives.* Typically, Peter has the store to himself, and that's how he likes it. He has no issues running it from orders to billings to updating the website and everything in between. It is a quiet oasis from the bustling city. He enjoys meeting people on his terms in the store. He can carry on conversations about literature and loves sharing his opinions with his clients and recommending books.

His thoughts deviate to the woman who's led him to this regression session. *What was her name? Clare. That's it.* She was so passionate about the past life thing. He finds himself wishing she would come back. There was something about her he found very attractive. He has her email, but that would be too forward, he thinks. He's not that guy. That guy seems a bit creepy. That's a Sanderson thing to do. If fate had them meet again, he would welcome it and ask her out, PTSD or not.

Peter purchases a sausage from a street vendor to fill the void before his session, remembering what Theresa had said: *that there was no time limit.* He catches the mostly deserted bus to head up to the Grosse Pointe Woods neighborhood and watches the world blur through the tinted picture windows. People hurry along the sidewalk to their next destination, not giving each other a second glance.

He'd enlisted to protect these people who ignore their fellow man in the great race to best them by rushing up the rungs of the social and financial hierarchy. He doesn't bemoan them their right to embrace capitalism. He joined the military to fight for that privilege. But something is lost on them. They're not necessarily embracing it for the right reasons, he thinks. But he's always seen that. He sees that now in Sanderson. *Fat and free. That's what capitalism affords you if you're willing to put in the hard work.* Peter tends to lean slightly to the left, maintaining a healthy distrust of authority and a well-maintained physique. Tonight, he hopes to begin the journey to a healthy mind.

Peter disembarks the bus with two or three others just before Theresa's Street. It's a good twenty-five-minute ride from the store. He checks his phone for the time. He can walk the remaining distance in five minutes easily. It's a crisp evening. June can prove cooler than Peter likes, but at least the spring rains have tapered off some, and he's dressed for the weather. His mind wanders again as the scent of pine lining the well-treed street ignites memories. He's a boy. His father has been away for months, and his mother sits in the front yard with him, reading her book while he plays on the lawn.

It's not a particularly important memory. This happened quite a bit in the summers. Peter's family moved a lot with his father's military career, and it was rare he had any friends to connect with. When school began, he would find one or two other army brats who might relate. The familiarity he's experiencing is unnerving, but he concedes it's just the scent caught up in the wind illuminating his memories. Nothing more.

At Theresa's home, he rings the bell, and she opens the door. Peter notices she wears a pleasant enough smile, but it seems skewed. She'd greeted him with a similar one the day before. He wonders briefly what had put her smile on the defensive like this. Her features are symmetrical and pleasing to the eye. All but her smile. He's read about how people's faces have a happy and a sad side. He'd witnessed this same trend on his own after reading about it. Perhaps Theresa's is just more pronounced? Whatever the reason, he shakes off the thought and greets her with his own tentative smile.

Chapter 7

Theresa leads Peter into the treatment room after hanging his light jacket on the hook provided. She's excited to get started. Peter looks a bit on edge, but he's probably just nervous.

Theresa turns to Peter and asks, "how was your day?" She directs him to the lounge with her hand, and Peter sits, his hands pressed together between his thighs.

"Not very noteworthy," Peter stares at his hands. He's wringing them again. "My boss stopped in first thing and stayed the day."

"Is he the owner of the shop?" Theresa pulls her plush leather chair closer to the lounge and sits.

"Yes, well, his ex-wife," Peter looks around the room, and Theresa activates the light dimmer from her pendant. Peter is preoccupied, she thinks.

"Is it nice to have the company? I haven't been in a proper bookstore in years. I imagine them mostly empty."

"That's how I like it," Peter replies and situates himself horizontally on the lounge. "I-is this right? Do I lie down?"

"Yes," Theresa affirms, indicating the weighted blankets. "If you'd feel more comfortable with a blanket drawn over you, please take one." He tests the different weights and decides on the 20 lb. He looks pleased with his choice.

"I've never slept with a weighted blanket." He tells her, shifting his weight under it. "I think I like this."

"Good, though you won't fall asleep here, you will become aware that you are extremely relaxed. I find the blankets assist in the transformation." She sits back and explains that she will record the session for future reference and activates the app on her phone.

"Your boss, what's his name?" Theresa asks. "Sanderson, Mr. Sanderson," Peter tells her, eyes shut. "Is Mr. Sanderson a source of stress for you?"

Peter shrugs, nestling into the pillow. "I've never experienced my dissociative fugue from interactions with him or anything."

"Oh, have you experienced lost time before?" She makes a note of this.

"I've only lost time twice before," Peter is quick to answer. "Probably not a big deal. Once following the event in Kandahar and once more state-side a few days after returning." Peter explains that his psychiatrist believed his dissociative fugue occurred to present a means of escape from his stressors. "Losing time like that scares me," he continues, "but I haven't experienced it since."

"Good. I ask about your boss because he may take precedence over other events if you are experiencing stressors from recent memory. If that's the case, we'll manage those first and move on to your main triggers." Theresa further dims the lights and explains the processes that will place him in a trance-like state as gently as possible and in a muted tone. Peter nods and looks quite content.

Theresa begins by offering reiki to even out Peter's energy, focusing it for the hypnosis. She does this with all her clients so they may experience the most benefit from the regression therapy. She closes her eyes and places her hands just above the blanket, never touching Peter. She scans his body's energy by moving her hands over him. Reiki will identify any energy needing to be directed, and Theresa will guide it away from Peter. Once she is satisfied, she begins to speak to him in whispers. The phone doesn't need to pick up this portion of the session. What's important is to record the past life or lives that will announce themselves through Peter's narration.

Eyes may be the windows to the soul, but doors open experiences the soul has encountered. Theresa describes this concept to Peter, guiding him through a long hallway. Doors will appear to Peter's left and right next, materializing as he moves through the hall in his mind's eye. Peter rests heavily in the lounge now, eyes closed.

"Choose a door, Peter. Where you enter, you will realize a past life that will assist you in this life." Theresa allows him the time to make a choice. She knows each will appear different in its architecture and color. Some will be shiny, while others will seem faded. The textures will vary. A combination of these things will draw him to the life his soul recalls with a lesson that can help him navigate the here and now.

"It's a tall door with bars," Peter explains what he sees and where he's going at Theresa's request. "I'm pushing it open... it's dark. There are bars all around me. I'm in prison. It's cold... I don't like it."

Theresa interrupts. "Stay with this life, Peter. It's a gift. You're experiencing it now because it has a message for you. Remember this isn't happening to you presently." She watches as the hairs on Peter's forearm prick up. He's reacting to the stimuli. She admits the process borders on the paranormal, and though Peter is under hypnosis, he's very aware of her and what she's saying.

"It's cold," he repeats.

"Let's step back a few years in this life, Peter. Tell me your name," Theresa's suggestion will build a deeper story to draw from.

"They call me Martin," he says, shifting slightly in the lounge. He sighs. "It's warm now. My bare feet are in a creek to cool off. I've made a fishing rod out of a stick and some twine."

Peter describes his life as a young African American boy in the heart of the south in the United States. Georgia, he asserts. Life had never been easy for his family. They felt unwelcome. Constantly on edge, fearful for their lives. To enjoy a moment like this in Walton County was a blessed one.

Peter feels compelled to advance years living as Martin Dorsey, drafted into the US Army to fight the growing threat overseas. Nazis. He's read the papers and admits he's terrified to face them but understands repression and is proud to stand up to it, even if it's on another continent.

He shifts further into the future and explains his apprehension over the scene in front of him. Shells are exploding all around. He's part of the Italian campaign. His segregated platoon of African Americans has fought bravely. The Apennines mountains loom in the distance but fade to black as smoke and dust rise from the bombardment of mortars slamming into the naked earth around him. Trees are cracked and splintered. The colored infantry supports the 1st armored division, who press forward despite the shelling.

Again, Peter feels the pull of time. He's back where he started. Walton County. His mother is happy to see him. His sisters as well. He's glad to be home but disappointed in how he and his colored comrades are treated even after serving their country. Unrest in the southern states is coming to a head. Martin supports the civil rights movements. White supremacists are rallying to take back their power and resent African Americans' potential to vote and be recognized as equals. Lynching is becoming alarmingly commonplace in Georgia. Martin – *Peter* conveys his concern to Theresa.

A moment later, Peter returns to prison.

Theresa asks him what year it is, and he answers 1946.

"Look at your feet, Peter. Tell me what you're wearing."

"I'm not wearing anything." Peter's head tilts slightly in the lounge. "It's a cell. There are chains around my ankles. My hands are cuffed as well. But I don't deserve this. I haven't done anything to deserve this." Theresa notices his body shake and lays a calming hand on his chest.

"Then why are you in prison? Is there a guard? What are they wearing?" She wants him to focus.

"Yes, he's a big, white man with a sarcastic smile. He wears a blue uniform... a double-breasted jacket - a gold badge on his left breast. There is a gun at his hip - a pistol. He's mocking me - my color. He tells me someone's coming for - coming for me. It'll be a lynching. They claim I raped a white woman. They say I did it, but I know I didn't. I explain it to the officer, but he calls me a wet rag as if I'm sucking all the fun out of this - whatever *this* is."

"Focus, Peter," Theresa asks him to concentrate on the officer's eyes. Identifying this man from the past could lead Peter to an individual in his current life, one who is causing levels of anxiety and unrest. "What this man is doing, taunting you like that, it's not right. You don't deserve it. It's cruel."

"Lights are coming closer. Torches. I see them through the bars in the window." Peter is visibly agitated. Theresa senses the scene he's recalling will have a bad

46

end. "The officer is at the door and pulling me out! He says it's time for me to pay the piper." Peter's voice is animated. He explains to Theresa how he resists, and more men in white cloaks pour into the small station, dragging him out into the night. A noose lowers over his head, and when secured around his neck, he is pulled along the dirt road. He struggles against the rough rope with his fingers trying to stay upright, but a man on a horse has the end of the rope now and moving too fast for him to keep up. He fights to breathe, and this is reflected in his narration.

When they stop, the men form a circle around him, each with a torch, and he is brought to his feet under a low-hanging branch of a sturdy Oak. "This is it," Peter tells her, anxiety sticks in his throat. "This is how it happens. This is how I die." Theresa watches on as tears escape down Peter's reddening cheeks. This is a difficult life that somehow connects him to his current difficulties.

"I can't stop them. I'm helpless. I'm terrified. Don't let them lynch me. Please," he says pleadingly.

Theresa needs Peter to live the life through to its conclusion but doesn't want him to suffer this end. Not again. That he is anxious always makes for a difficult transition.

Theresa can appreciate the urgency in Peter's tone, "tell me who the officer is. Tell me. You know him in the present. He's followed you here." Theresa is on the edge of her seat and needs Peter to identify the individual causing him grief in this life to address it.

"I do know him," Peter announces, head slowly nodding. His body relaxes under the weight of the blanket, and he offers a name. *Sanderson.* Peter's boss. She considers this information and decides it is enough that he has made the connection and pulls him out of the experience.

Peter opens his eyes as directed and slowly emerges from the past. "It's Sanderson," he whispers, a hand instinctively stroking his throat. He turns to Theresa. "How can that be?"

"You mentioned him before we began," she reminds him. "You don't like him, and for good reason. He's hurt you in the past. His presence in your life now is triggering your PTSD."

Peter pushes himself up on the lounge. "But my whole life is in that bookstore. My apartment, my job."

"And now you have a choice to make, Peter. Do you continue to work and live in a place where this man only serves to increase your anxieties, or do you move on?"

Peter frowns deeply. "I've nowhere else to go. I'm making a life for myself there."

"You'll weigh your options," Theresa tells him, cautious not to upset him further. "You'll decide whether you can manage his presence in your life or not. That you've come away with this information is a good start."

"Seems more like an end," Peter shifts his legs off the lounge and pushes the blanket aside. "The man frustrates me, but I don't know that he's a trigger."

"I'm afraid the cycle won't be broken until you divest yourself from him. You're twenty-eight now."

"Yes?"

"You were the same age in the past you just experienced. It's a pattern. Peter. I've seen it before."

"A pattern? Like, you mean he's come back to hurt me again?"

"Yes, he's what I call a repeat past life offender where others are benevolent or helpful." She looks at the time. He's been under for just over an hour. She doesn't feel he could manage another life tonight.

"So, people repeatedly stick to you and reappear to torment you?" Peter looks forlorn.

"Souls, yes." She admits it's a dark take on the experience, but it's predominantly been hers. "Some are here to help you along while others make life difficult. It doesn't seem fair, I know. Life isn't fair. You understand that. But if we can use this knowledge to move you out of Sanderson's circle of influence, then you're getting ahead."

"I can't see myself leaving what I've built," Peter wrings his hands. "It's a lot to take in."

"You can learn to live with someone who doesn't have your best interests in mind," Theresa explains. "Use the tools you have when he's around. Practice your breathing exercises. Keep crystals nearby."

"Crystals?" Peter's expression shows hesitation.

"Yes, clear quartz, for example, will deflect negativity." She stands and moves to her collection of crystals and picks up a palm-sized quartz. She hands it to Peter, who reluctantly holds it in his hands.

"What's something like this cost?"

"This one I'm giving you. I'd like you to keep this on you or near you when dealing with your Mr. Sanderson."

"Thank you," he moves the many-edged crystal around in his hands. "That's kind of you."

"I think we'll end our session tonight and let you ruminate on your past. I'll send you the recording via text."

Peter stands and places the quartz in his hoodie pocket. Theresa asks him if he is alert enough to walk. He studies his feet a moment and nods. She accepts his payment via e-transfer and, at the door, smiles and gently leads him out. The night is cool but clear. Peter thanks her for her time, and Theresa asks him if the following week works for his next session.

When Peter is gone, Theresa sits heavily on the couch. His session has affected her energy tonight, and she wishes he would remove himself from the toxic relationship with his boss. Peter is clearly invested in his life there and seems unwilling to take the necessary steps to remove himself. Still, it is his choice, but the anxiety she has inherited over the experience stays with her. She snaps up the cylindrical-shaped clear quartz that adorns a side table and rubs it between her palms.

Chapter 8

Peter returns to his apartment above the bookshop to find the lights still on in the store. Anxiety rises in his chest. *Sanderson must still be here.* He approaches the front glass door and looks in. Beyond the counter, he sees the man slumped over the desk in the office. *Fuck.* This guy must be in deep with the wife, he thinks. *How many more days and nights would he spend here?*

Peter tries the door. It's unlocked. That's dangerous. The neighborhood isn't, necessarily, but he knows that an unlocked shop door is an invitation to thieves. He opens the door slowly so as not to set off the hanging bell and slips in, locking the latch. Sanderson stirs. Peter creeps around the store to make sure no one else is inside. He moves stealthily through one aisle after another, covering the storefront in under a minute. Then he checks behind the counter and then the storeroom. He picks up the wooden bat leaning against the wall and slips into the small basement turning on the light. No one here either. His heart is racing. *What a fool of a man to get blackout drunk and leave the shop unprotected.* The office lamp shows Sanderson's head resting on one of the rare books he'd brought with him. Peter thinks next to his apartment and moves up the staircase and into his home. After a brief look around, he counts his lucky stars to find nothing out of place and wonders whether to wake the boss or let him sleep off the drink.

Another day of sharing the same space does not sit well with Peter. Perhaps he should look for another apartment and another job, but this stirs a panic attack. He paces the floors and shakes out the anxiety building in his arms. The images of those Afghan children assault his memory. Their innocent faces often accompany these attacks. They should have been allowed to live. It's a crime he couldn't save them. He wrings his hands as he paces. Think, he tells himself. *Breathe. Just breathe.* The attack subsides, as they do, within a few minutes, and he's left to contemplate his future.

Then he hears a bang, and Sanderson bellows from below. This is not your problem, Peter tells himself. Just go to bed. He looks at his phone and realizes it's only 8 pm. Then he gets a notification and see's Theresa's text with the audio file attached from his session. Does he want to relive that again? No. He thanks her and confirms his next appointment in a week. The idea that the lout downstairs could be the same man who allowed an angry mob to hang him in 1946 is astonishing. That he's still an asshole in this life isn't difficult to believe, but will he never learn? Again, not his problem. He considers looking for a new apartment and realizes he's tied into this lease for another three months. Maybe he can find a new job, though.

He picks up his tablet and begins a search. The process is discouraging. Big box bookstores are accepting applications for the roll, but for much less money. He slams the tablet down and decides to ride out this job until his lease ends. The sound alerts the oaf below, and Sanderson yells up the stairs.

"You up there, Banks!?" He sounds like a spiteful child in the throes of a temper tantrum. "Get down here!" Peter contemplates whether he will take Sanderson up on the demand. His head drops, and he stands, inhaling deeply, the air exiting his mouth in a long sigh. Then he approaches his open door and starts down the stairs.

"Can I help you?" He asks solemnly, meeting the flushed Sanderson at the bottom of the stairs. He's very drunk.

"Can you *help me?* What the fuck kind of a question is that?"

"You're shouting."

"I'll shout all I want. It's my shop!" Sanderson uses the wall to hold up his heavy frame. "I need you to do something for me." He's pointing his fat finger at Peter, eyes closing hard as if trying to remember his request. Peter waits while the blood pounds against his temples.

"I'm not on the clock. It's after eight," Peter points out.

"Do you *want* a job in the morning?" He threatens.

Peter acquiesces and sighs. "What do you need?" He says pointedly. The smell of alcohol is ripe, coming off the fat man. He reeks of it. Something must really be wrong at home.

"I need you to run to the corner store and pick me up a bottle of whisky." Sanderson is swaying as he says this.

"You don't think you've had enough?"

Sanderson's gaze burns through Peter, and his expression reminds Peter of an angry boar. "I didn't ask your opinion."

"No, but I'm not going to do that." He wonders whether he ought to though and let the fool drink himself to death.

Sanderson straightens himself, his belly untucking his dress shirt from his pants. The man looks distressed. "Fine, you're fired." He waves a dismissive hand.

"You can't fire me for this," Peter explains calmly, but he doesn't feel calm. He feels irate over the idea this entitled prick thinks he has such power over him. Peter tries to keep his cool but senses that it may be an exercise in futility. His hands form fists as he fights back urges to throttle the drunk.

"Get out of my shop!" Sanderson bellows. Peter turns and moves back up the stairs to his apartment. "Get *out*, I said!" Sanderson obviously sees the two as connected.

"My apartment isn't the shop. I'm going to bed. Sleep off your day drinking, and we'll talk in the morning." But Peter doesn't expect him to remember this interaction in the morning. Peter won't forget it, though. He continues up the stairs and shuts and locks his door.

"You son of a bitch!" Sanderson lumbers up the staircase and begins banging on Peter's door. "You'll never work in this town again!" More threats from the arrogant asshole. *Who thinks they have that kind of power?* Peter goes to his bedroom and shuts the door to cancel out the bloated idiot's shouts. *I could surprise him by opening the door and pushing him down the stairs.* Rather than act out his fantasy, he lays in bed practicing his breathing until Sanderson gives up, and Peter eventually drifts off.

The following morning Peter descends the stairs with his coffee and another for Sanderson. A peace offering should he have any recollection of the night before, but his boss is nowhere to be found.

"Good riddance." Peter places both cups on the counter and moves to unlock the front door. It is, of course, already unlocked. Sanderson must have rushed out in the night, leaving his shop unprotected. Peter shakes his head and begins his day.

No angry texts or emails are forthcoming, so he assumes he'd gone home and forgotten the whole ordeal. Just as well, Peter thinks. He can't even remember the last time Sanderson called or texted him. *Do I even have his number?* They interact via the store's email and the rare visits he makes to the shop, and neither has amounted to much – if any, in the past few months. The bell over the front door chimes, interrupting Peter's conversation with himself, and Clare, who had nudged him to see Theresa walks back into his life.

"Hello again," she says cheerily. She hadn't been so animated on their first encounter; he thinks and smiles optimistically at her.

"You're back," he manages, "it's good to see you again. How can I help?" Then he remembers what he'd told himself; if she resurfaced, he would ask her out. This information sets his nerves on edge.

"I think I've found my new happy place," she says, looking around the shop.

"Oh? Good," Peter's hands are sweating. He stands at attention. Rigid. "I, um, take it you mean the bookshop?"

She smiles her playful smile and pushes up her oversized designer glasses. "Yes, I have decided that I like it here. The smell of the books and the variety, and the dim lighting. And the company."

Peter is surprised to hear this. He hadn't thought she was into him. "I'm happy to hear it," he replies, unsure how to carry this conversation forward.

Clare holds her handbag tight against her chest and then opens it to reveal a sheet of paper. "I'd like you to order me these books next, please." Peter takes the list and studies it. She could have emailed him the list.

"More of the same, it sounds like?" He looks up, and she nods once, still with that elfin smile. Peter senses a clandestine subtext pass over her expression.

"More so, I'd like to ask you to dinner." She nods again. It's cute, Peter thinks, how she nods after she says something encouraging him to nod as well.

"That's, uh," very forward, he thinks, but he'll take it. "Honestly, you beat me to the punch. I had told myself I would ask you out if or when you returned."

"Oh, that's kismet, isn't it!" It wasn't a question. "Serendipity even." She laughs in a halting way that further endears her to Peter.

"I think they mean the same thing!" Peter laughs with her. "I'm free tonight if you'd like to stop by the shop again at 6?"

"That will do nicely," Clare replies. "I have a place in mind if you don't have any objections to the woman taking the lead."

"You've been doing just fine so far," Peter replies, and she laughs again. Peter feels a further connection to Clare in how they carry the conversation effortlessly now.

"Then I'll see you tonight!" Another nod, and she adjusts her glasses again, zips her handbag, and turns to leave but stops herself from looking back at Peter. "Dress business casual; it's not high-end, but it's nice." Peter nods, and she slips out the front door.

Peter walks to the picture window and watches her move down the sidewalk. His chest warms with hope, but his inherent skepticism rarely takes a backseat to optimism. *Could she really like him? Would his PTSD stomp on his chances? Would she see through his veneer?* Regardless of his waning self-confidence, this is a nice affirmation that life doesn't have to be all doom and gloom after last night's trials.

Chapter 9

Detective William Harlow is called from his desk to visit a crime scene under strict orders to keep the press at a distance. This is a common enough request, but rarely is it cited. It' Arriving on the scene, Harlow finds himself in one of Detroit's most affluent neighborhoods, Palmer Woods. He flashes his badge at the manned gate and drives through the winding boulevard and up the driveway that could easily accommodate ten cars. A good thing too, he thinks, as there is a heavy police presence here already.

He spots two cruisers, a forensics van, another unmarked car like his own, and an ambulance. Uniformed officers, paramedics, and firefighters are busily moving about their vehicles. Harlow was told there had been a murder, but not just a murder; this one had all the signs of becoming something much more. This information intrigues him. This morning, the call came from a distraught son who had found his father deceased on the premises. Harlow had reviewed the 911 call earlier. The voice on the call was experiencing genuine shock. Grief over his find was palpable.

Harlow steps out of his car and asks the paramedics how their day is going as they loiter at the back of the ambulance.

"Another day, another body," the tall woman tells him. Harlow likes dark humor. It's something police, firefighters and paramedics share. It helps first responders cope. You've got to desensitize yourself to the horrors of the job. It's not disrespectful. It's proactive. "When you're done, we'll take it to the coroner." He nods and ducks, moving through the half-open garage door.

The scene is difficult to walk into. He sympathizes with the boy who made the call. A suicide by all accounts, but then that's the easy call. He was brought in to read the note. What he finds rather than a standard *'I can't do it anymore, I'm sorry,'* he would describe more as a calling card than a suicide letter because that's precisely what it is. Now he understands why his captain reminded him to keep reporters at bay with this one. This wasn't something they wanted to get out. This was big, and it had the potential to get out of control quickly.

"Detective," a young constable approaches Harlow with a frown that supports the gravity of the scene. Harlow wonders whether this is his first and how many lines will be carved into his youthful face over the next ten years. "You've seen the note."

Harlow nods, holding the evidence in its plastic baggie. It's a clear statement. Short and sweet. Confusing? Yes, but it looks like it was created on a digital printer with 100 lb. paper by the feel of it. No handwriting. Maybe there are fingerprints to pull off the paper. Unlikely. They'd know soon enough.

"Thank you for securing the scene, Constable," Harlow says. The young man grunts his reply. "Is the family here? The boy who made the call?"

"Yes, sir. They're in the back sunroom. Wife and child." The constable leads the detective into the expansive sitting room overlooking a pristine, landscaped yard with an inground pool that reminds Harlow more of a resort than a backyard. "We've asked some preliminary questions but left it at their whereabouts last night and the usual."

"Okay, good," Harlow pats the man on the back and journeys into the space where the wife is comforting her son. The boy looks about 14, and the wife around 50. Even after all these years, he still feels uneasy interviewing victims. He pulls in a quick breath and releases it.

"Ma'am, son," he approaches them and sits on the coffee table, legs spread. "I'm Detective Harlow. I'm so sorry for your loss. Your husband was a pillar in the community." He says this assuming the dead man must have contributed in some way living in a house like this. Must have been important. Must have a lot of money too. If this was staged for the life insurance, Harlow would know within a few minutes. He was good at his job and could sense a lie a mile away.

"Thank you for coming," the woman says, a tissue at her petite nose. A trophy wife perhaps, but shedding real tears. "We're at a loss. Frederick wasn't a man who would take his own life. He just wouldn't." She says this passionately, her gaze insisting he catch her husband's murderer. *That's interesting.*

"You found your father in the garage this morning at 7:45 am?" He shifts his attention to the boy. He's still in his pajamas, and his nose and eyes are red. The boy nods, his head down. "I'm sorry you found him like this. Your mother doesn't believe he would do this himself."

"Why would he?" The boy agrees. "We have a soccer meet this afternoon. *Had.* He wouldn't do... *that.*" He points angrily behind them toward the front of the house.

"No, of course," he looks to the wife, "do you have a home security camera? We might discover what happened quickly with the footage." Harlow is running through the paces. He'd like to think the killer would be stupid, but since they had the forethought to leave a note, he fears that won't be the case.

"Yes, I've been scrolling through the data," she lifts her phone half-heartedly, "but nothing unusual."

"Please give your account information to the constable as we may discover something you missed." Upon closer inspection, something could turn up with experienced forensic eyes on the footage. She nods and turns to speak with the young constable.

"You found your father and called 911 immediately?" He asks the boy.

"Yes," he says solemnly. He's fighting back the tears, gulping down air. He's strong, but that resolve will break soon. Once everyone is gone, and they're left alone, he'll be a boy without a father.

"Nothing out of the ordinary last night? No noises you questioned. Shadows. Had your husband gone to bed with you?" Harlow directs his questions to the wife.

She snorts out a reply, "I can't remember the last time he slept in our bed. It's been forever."

"Mom," the boy says, accompanied by a troubled frown.

"It's true; we've been in a bad way the past year. He's gone a *lot.* His work takes him all over the world."

"So, when did he arrive home?" Harlow feels he is getting somewhere.

"The cameras say 2:30 am," she replies and blows her nose lightly.

"So, the last time you saw him alive," he looks at the boy apologetically and continues, "was when?"

The wife considers this and scrolls through her phone. "June 12. He was here for supper. Briefly."

"Okay, did he mention anything at all? Problems he was having with someone. Having met a stranger. An old friend. Anything you can pinpoint?"

"We didn't talk much. We text even less if you'd like my phone records."

"He did talk, mom; you just weren't *listening*," her son breaks in. "he said he was looking forward to the soccer meet today. He was going to come."

"Oh, sweetheart, you know he wouldn't have made it."

"He said he would,"

"And how many times have we heard that?"

Harlow is picking up the dynamic in the house. Spurned wife, hopeful kid, absentee husband, and father. Classic. The wife could have killed him, but to end up as he did... doesn't add up. Besides, poison is the go-to of disgruntled housewives.

He looks at the dead man's phone in his hand secured in a baggy, curious over the content, and says: "We will want all communications you've had with your husband in the last three months, so, please give the constable access to your plans' account." He looks kindly at the boy. "We'll ask for your son's as well."

"We want to cooperate in any way we can," she explains. "He was a better man than I'm making him out to be; I'm sorry." Emotions run high in these situations, and Harlow understands this. "I loved him; he just didn't have time for us. This is a big house with a lot of bills. He worked hard to give us all of this."

"Do you believe he was under a great deal of stress over it?"

She looks Harlow straight in the eye and holds his stare. "I know for a fact he would never do this to himself. We'd discussed the subject several times as my... my sister committed suicide years ago. We would never do that to each other and certainly not to Freddy Jr."

"I told you," Junior backs his mom up and blows his nose.

"We're canvassing your neighborhood, and we'll see if it produces anything we can use. Your camera footage and phone and email communications will be reviewed over the next few days. Standard procedure. You'll have a uniformed officer parked outside your house for your protection." Harlow stands. "For your safety, and if we need to ask more questions, please stay at home. Again, I'm sorry for your loss. We'll do everything in our power."

Harlow looks at Freddy Jr. and offers him a sympathetic smile and nod. Freddy's head falls again.

Harlow moves around the house, feeling out the crime scene. He looks at the printer and paper in their home office. He marks down the make and serial number and the thickness of the stock. Next, he looks for signs of a struggle, broken baubles, and scuff marks on the floor. Nothing. The doors, all five of them, weren't forced open. Windows look clean.

The forensics team is busy in the garage where the body was found and the victim's car, checking for prints and fibers, hair and spit, and blood. He'll get their report in a few days. He moves outside and studies the camera placement. The doorbell is one. There is another at the side of the house lacking the four-car garage and another overlooking the beautiful backyard. Motion lights adorn both sides of the house.

Whoever the killer is who left their calling card was a pro. But what is the motive? The rich tend to make more enemies than friends in Harlow's experience with the elite. It could be a long list. His friends, enemies, partners, and extended family will all be interviewed in their time. The paramedics see this as a suicide, so there shouldn't be any leaks to the media there. The firefighters left long ago. The press would sensationalize the killing and build their own stories, either scaring the perp into hiding, inflating their ratings, or both. So, the note must be kept a secret. No one can know.

Harlow spends the remainder of the day at the scene, conferring with forensics, making notes, and snapping pictures with his phone. He watches the body be bagged and removed from the premises, and the ambulance slowly leave the scene.

After a brief return to the office, he goes home, where a bottle of bourbon and an empty condo welcome him back. The ex-wife took the dog, Oscar, a dachshund they'd bought five years ago. He loved that dog, but she had a real spitfire for an attorney, and he'd lost more than half of their assets. The condo was a good move for him after the drama; no yard, no maintenance, no nothing.

Harlow pulls the cork from the bourbon and pours himself three fingers over cold stones. Ice weakens the bourbon and robs it of its full flavor. The stones were a gift from his ex-wife. Tiff hadn't taken these, at least, he thinks. She never was one for the hard stuff, though.

After two of these, Harlow rolls up his sleeve to expose the charred flesh of his left forearm. Then he picks up a lighter next to a set of candles he's never lit and strikes the flint. The fire burns brightly, and he moves the flame under his tortured forearm.

Pain is a funny thing; he reflects on this as the underside of his forearm screams for him to stop. The smoke stinks of burning flesh, but no hair is left to catch fire. Harlow flinches, taking his thumb off the lighter. Pain can be felt both externally and internally. Surely, when his wife left him, he had suffered complications concurrent with someone falling out of love with him internally. The questions, the what-ifs, the heartbreak, and sadness all lived inside him. It was his fault, she'd clarified. He accepted her explanation and allowed her to take what she wanted. They say if you love someone, let them go. They don't mention the sense of loss that accompanies that decision. Eventually, the sadness dissipated, and he became stoic over it, feeling nothing. That didn't sit right with him. So, he decided to play out the pain externally; and the self-harm began.

The thing about self-harm is that it's addictive. Connecting with his pain gives him purpose. It gives him control. A part of him wants the pain back. A part of him wants Tiff back.

Chapter 10

Peter appreciates punctuality, and Clare's arrival at the bookstore is just that. Six o'clock on the dot. He'd become preoccupied imagining an evening with her outside the bookstore. It's been an excellent distraction from his usual routine; living in the present rather than regretting his past or feeling anxious over his future. Peter greets her with a smile and a small gift.

"Oh, you needn't have done that, Peter." She accepts the box and opens it. "Oh, did you want me to wait or..."

"No, it's nothing," it isn't nothing, he tells himself and corrects the course, "it's fine, please," Peter urges her to open the box. He chews the end of his thumb, watching her eyes as they fall on the book inside.

"Oh, my, it's beautiful," she says, looking up at Peter, her mouth pulling up into a satisfied smile. Clare pulls the book from the box and studies the hardcover. "How did you find this?"

"When I ordered from your list, I saw that we had this edition in the safe." He feels proud to be able to give her something as intimate as a book. Well, intimate to a lover of books, anyway.

"It's just lovely, really," her hands caress the spine, opening it. "What a nice surprise. You didn't have to."

"Don't worry; I paid for it." They laugh. "When it popped up on the screen, I couldn't believe it. It's kismet. *Again.*"

"It is." Clare's cheeks redden. "It just makes this evening all the more special. Thank you so much." She looks for what to do with the gift, and Peter offers a solution.

"You don't have to carry it around all night. I'll put it back in the safe, and you can pick it up later." She hands it back gently as if it's a priceless relic.

"Tonight then, we'll come back tonight. I've had fantasies over spending time in a bookstore like this after hours."

"Oh, confession time," Peter kids. "I'm living out my fantasy working here."

"Look at us, sharing our fantasies in the first five minutes." They laugh again. "I think you'll really enjoy where I'm taking you tonight."

"I am at your mercy."

Clare moistens her lips with a thin, pink tongue and smiles shyly, pushing her glasses higher on her nose. "Then let's be on our way. My car is just parked on the street a block away."

Peter locks the shop, and they walk past the sparse collection of people as they exit and enter the bus. He again feels a rush of familiarity with Clare. They're so comfortable in each other's presence. It's refreshing. He considers taking her hand; the urge is incredible. Peter likens the sensation to two magnets trying desperately to draw together.

"How was your day?" she asks.

"Small talk, I can do that too." Peter smiles down at her, and she up at him.

"No, I'm honestly interested. There's a sense of fascination bookstores hold for me."

"Alright, it was a good day, actually. I sold somewhere in the vicinity of thirty books, two special editions, and one rare find," he winks, indicating that was the book he bought.

"Is it hard to sustain a bookstore like that in this day and age?" Clare roots around in her handbag.

"It's coming back - the brick and mortar. Today was a light day, to be honest. People are social animals. Like the big malls never died out, bookstores are experiencing a kind of renaissance."

"I love hearing that. I honestly feared they would all disappear!" She stops and hits the button on her key fob. "This is me."

Her car is a Tesla. It's beautiful. She opens the passenger side door for Peter. "Well, this is nice. Thank you!" They laugh, and Clare shakes her head.

As they drive away, Clare notes, "This place isn't far, but it's kind of pricey."

"If you're opening doors for me, I'll assume you're picking up the tab, win-win." Clare chuckles at that. Peter likes the way the conversation is flowing. He likes himself in her presence, feeling his confidence rise with each witty exchange.

The conversation never lags between them and remains like this all evening through dinner at the trendy 'Quoth the Raven', where Peter learns books can act as impressive decoration just as well as entertainment. They sit at a high table just beyond the lounge where aristocratic-looking people enjoy the gothic architecture concurrent with Poe's writings, sipping their pink ladies, whiskeys, and ales. There is a theme to the place that resonates with him, as Clare knew it would. It's an expansive restaurant segmented into story-specific spaces. They are seated in the coveted *The Raven* section, where there are several more named after Poe's works like *A Telltale Heart, The House of Usher, The Murders in the Rue Morgue,* and more. Each section is decorated according to the author's imagination and remains cohesive throughout. The thought behind the place is impressive, Peter thinks. Dinner offers a similar experience; the menu items are cleverly described using a play on words that reminds one of Poe's literary stylings – unique and dark. Peter orders the Chicken schnitzel platter, *pounded flat with punishing impunity.*

Between them, Peter and Clare manage to discuss the finer points of Poe's ability to shift his readers to a demented point of view and his use of language and symbolic play on the meanings of words. Clare is the perfect woman for Peter, he thinks as he carves into his crispy chicken schnitzel.

They enjoy a Cognac each to end the experience as it's considered Poe's favorite drink, which leads into a discussion about the author's notorious drinking habit, which contributed to his early death at 40.

"Imagine Poe reincarnated," Clare says, trailing a finger up her cognac glass where a trickle has escaped. She places the finger in her mouth, and Peter watches her lips part to receive the fugitive drop. "He could be here, amongst us!" Clare says animatedly. Peter finds the idea of it exhilarating as well, having never given any thought to such a claim before. He finds himself smitten with Clare's enthusiasm.

"It could keep you up nights," Peter suggests, "considering the lives lived in a room like this."

"That guy," Clare points out a man two tables over as tactfully as she can. "The one with the magnificent beard. I wonder who he was in a past life."

"Rasputin," Peter jokes, lips pinched together in thought. "Lover of the Russian queen!"

Clare nearly spits out her cognac; a hand pressing against her lips conceals the outburst. "Oh, my god, that's so Rasputin!" She says through her fingers.

Peter loves that he can make Clare laugh. She always lifts one delicate hand to her mouth as she does. "How about the woman at the bar. The one standing there waiting for a drink," Peter offers up their next target with a subtle nod.

"Hmm," Clare deliberates a moment, "The Russian queen?" She nods her nod and smiles impishly at Peter.

He raises his hands, and they fall to the table comically. "They don't even know each other in this life!"

"It's cruel, really," Clare adds, "Not ten feet apart, and they've no idea." She shakes her head joylessly, and then Peter watches her eyes sparkle to life as an idea corrupts her senses. "We should introduce them!"

"Oh, I'm not that forward," Peter admits, hands raised again, but defensively this time. He hates approaching strangers unless he's on his turf. "Besides, we can't affect their fates."

"Fate is fate," Clare returns. "Maybe we're supposed to interject. We could be part of their larger plan."

Clare's suggestion isn't lost on Peter, but his hands begin to sweat at the thought all the same. He spreads his palms over his jeans and feels anxious energy envelop him. He was never like this before Afghanistan, and it's becoming a real problem.

Clare reaches across the table and asks for Peter's hand. He offers it, and she places it between both of hers. Her hands are cool but soft. His are boiling now and wet.

"I'm just kidding, Peter," she admits. "I'm not going to force you." She looks at him with mock empathy from those big, hazel eyes hidden behind her stylish glasses. "But I think it would be a good team-building exercise for us."

"Team-building, eh?" Peter laughs it off but considers the story value if they were to attempt such a feat. Then what if they did look into each other's eyes and sense a connection? Could he rob them of that?

"Also, I'm feeling a bit adventurous tonight," her well-maintained brows raise once, twice, three times, exaggerating her interest.

"You're relentless," Peter replies with a smile he feels raising the right side of his face. He shakes his head imperceptibly, but Clare notices. "How do we do it?"

"Oh! We order a drink for her and say it's from Rasputin!" She's leaning into the center of the table on her forearms, and now he's doing the same. Their faces are inches apart.

"Okay, but we don't say *Rasputin*, right?"

"Right, right, that's probably not his name in this life." Her brows sinch in together, mocking the serious nature of their game.

"Right, so can you get his name, and I'll watch where she ends up?"

Clare stands abruptly, winks at Peter, and carries her cognac with her to Rasputin's table. Peter watches as she introduces herself. Oh, it looks like a case of mistaken identity. She's good, he thinks. She returns to their table and sits.

"Max. His name is Max," she says proudly with a nod confirming her information.

"That was brilliant," Peter says, feeling a little flush from the second-hand embarrassment over her brashness. "Okay, I'll order at the bar and have them send the drink."

At the bar, Peter asks the bartender, whose majestic mustache is perfectly twisted up at the ends, what the tall woman at that table – he points her out – just bought. The man tells him two whiskey sours, and Peter orders another to be delivered.

"Who shall I say is buying?"

"Max, but that's not me; it's the gentleman with the long beard right there," He points out Rasputin, a lie taking shape. "We're all old friends, and I don't think they've noticed one another yet. I want it to be a surprise." Peter winks at the bartender and leaves a 20 for the drink and tip. It's generous, but the barkeep needs to sell it if this is to work. "Trust me; you'll be doing them a real service. Keep me out of it, though."

Peter walks back to his seat, delighted with his role in seeing the diabolical plan take shape, wondering how this woman had convinced him to participate so easily.

"It's done," he tells her, picking up his cognac and sipping excitedly, watching the bartender walk to the queen's table, present the drink and point out Rasputin.

"Oh, my god," Clare has both hands over her mouth. "It's working!" They giggle and watch the Russian queen look past her girlfriend and wave subtly at

Rasputin. He notices her wave and looks about him, curious whether the tall woman is waving at him.

As Rasputin waves back with a raised eyebrow and a sinister smile, Peter and Clare can barely contain their glee.

"Holy shit," Clare can't stop smiling. "Peter, Peter," she grabs his arm, slapping it lightly, and Peter turns to see what she's seeing.

Rasputin rises from his chair, excuses himself from his table of two men who don't share his penchant for beards and walks confidently to the queen's table.

"It's happening," Peter says, gobsmacked.

Rasputin introduces himself to both women and then focuses on the queen. They share a smile and some words which seem pleasant enough.

"Oh, shit," Peter exclaims. "He's pulling out his phone. I think they're exchanging numbers!"

"This is fate," Clare announces matter-of-factly, her hands slamming down upon the table. "We just affected fate!"

Peter finds it utterly fascinating that their actions may have reconnected a distant relationship from over a hundred years ago. But whatever comes of this experiment, they've put the two together.

Clare lets out an audible sigh, clearly captivated by the results. "You know, they say there's no proof that Rasputin and Queen Alexandra had a romantic relationship," she says, her expression a unique combination of mischief and delight.

"We should write a paper on it," Peter suggests. "Follow them and track their experience. Then send them to Theresa for confirmation!"

"I love it!" Clare leans in again, and Peter feels a nervous flutter in his stomach. He finishes his cognac, and the bill arrives. True to her word, Clare snaps it up and pays with the mobile Tap.

The plan to stalk the Queen and Rasputin is abandoned, and they walk to the car, Peter thanking her for such a fun night.

The drive home is equally beguiling, and Peter considers his next move.

At the bookstore, they manage street parking right out front. Peter prays Sanderson hasn't taken it upon himself to use the shop as his hideaway again. The coast is clear.

"Any interest in a glass of red while you get your fantasy fix?" Peter teases. She agrees and asks to have her gift back. Peter retrieves the book and the wine. Two comfortable vintage high-back chairs face the one section of wall not cluttered with books. An electric fireplace is turned on. It completes the mood. Clare sighs as if she's found her happy place at last. Peter is thrilled. It's the most romantic thing he can imagine. Clare is stunning in the low light of the fireplace. Her high cheekbones are amplified as the shadows pull up her youthful face. She's a beautiful woman. He feels the urge to take her hand again. He wants her hands to caress him as they had the book he'd given her. The rush of the evening's shenanigans is fresh in his mind and grips his heart. He imagines many scenarios. While his imagination runs away, her soft lips connect with his.

After a long, deep kiss, they pull away from each other, Peter's lips feeling bruised from inexperience. "So, not just friends then?" Peter says with a playful smile rivaling hers. He's experiencing all the feels. She tells him to shut up and pulls him into her for another kiss.

Chapter 11

The following day finds Harlow interviewing family and friends of the deceased. They have been gracious enough to meet him at the Atwater St. station to review their whereabouts the night before and explain their relationship with the man. There are plenty of tears and genuine sadness, but not a lead amongst them. The perceived enemies and possible partners are being contacted now from his email, paper trail, and mobile contact list. The list spans continents. Presently, they are only interested in those contacts he's spent time with or spoken to over the past three months.

Harlow sees the last of the relatives out and stretches his back. The bandage on his forearm pulls at the tender, burned flesh hidden beneath his shirt sleeve. He scratches his head and looks at the latest casualties trapped in his ragged fingernails. His hair isn't long for this world, he thinks regrettably.

His captain asks him to join her in her office a moment later. He follows, admiring her form as she moves elegantly in her pencil skirt and tight-fitting blouse. She is young to have made captain, just a few years Harlow's senior. Her dark complexion and athletic frame create discord in Harlow. He respects her leadership qualities but fantasizes about how they might hook up. He does this often. He's been single for a while and made no effort to date. But fantasies are just that, and he doesn't deny himself their healing qualities.

"Preliminary autopsy is in. They didn't want us to wait for this information." She doesn't sit, so Harlow remains standing as well. She picks up a folder and hands it to him. Their fingers touch, and he questions whether she meant to do that. She is an attractive woman; straightened black, shoulder-length hair frames out her dark features intensifying the whites of her eyes. He flips the folder open and reads.

"An injection site," he reads aloud. "Orphenadrine." It's a paralyzing agent used for surgical procedures. "Then we're dealing with a murder and not a suicide."

Captain Anderson confirms this with a nod. "You'll be assigned this case as the lead investigator and follow up on any homicides, including a similar calling card. The FBI has been notified and will send a profiler to review our evidence." She notices Harlow's face fall. He can feel it.

"Don't get too territorial with the profiler. They're here to help." Her arms cross below her breasts. Harlow focuses on her large, round eyes.

"I'll be good," he smirks. "So, you believe this is the first in a series of killings?"

"The note," she says, "its only purpose is to let us know there's a killer in town. They clearly want the recognition for whatever reason."

"I guess I'd better do my homework on serial killers."

"The profiler will brief us when they arrive, but I won't discourage you from doing your own research." She rounds her desk and sits. "I hate to think we're wasting our time talking to his relatives and business partners, but we need to cover all avenues."

Harlow nods. "When can we expect the completed autopsy?"

"Within the next 24 hours, I'm told. Until then, continue your interviews and review with forensics what's turned up on the victim's phone and computers." She looks out her window which overlooks the Detroit River and the city of Windsor beyond it. "We can't shelve the idea that the note could be a distraction rather than a breadcrumb to the truth. His life insurance is requesting more information. I'm liaising with their investigator."

Harlow grunts, and she dismisses him. He sits in front of his computer and pulls up the victim's bank statements acquired earlier this morning. The victim has been on three trips in the last three months that took him overseas. Four more hotel stays appear where he remained on the continent. Lots of drinks at various hot spots within the city and a few tickets to sports venues. He was living his best life, but not in the eyes of his wife and child. *Why do people have wives and children if they aren't cut out to be family men?*

The new information about the needle is interesting, he ponders. He wasn't paralyzed off-site; the video clearly shows his car entering the garage. There is no camera footage of anyone else entering the home after that. So, did the wife stick him and carry out the murder or – Harlow pauses a moment, is it someone he'd met that night. Someone he might have snuck in.

Or did they follow him home? If they evaded the cameras, they knew where to go. *The victim let them in.* Maybe through the side door where the four-car garage lacks cameras? Maybe. Worth another look.

Harlow refers to where the victim has shopped regularly. He looks at everything. Nothing produces the gut reaction he tends to lean on.

There is a lot to wade through where this man is concerned. He was an active person. Maybe not with his family, but certainly on the road, in the bars, overseas. Texts seem unhelpful. All these contacts have been identified. No mistress he can find. No enemies demanding anything from him. Emails are business only. Social media doesn't exist for him save a business-related one. They will have to use bank statements to track his actions and whereabouts and follow up on each of them. It's arduous work but can be gratifying when done right. He'll visit the bar he ended up at the night of his murder. Perhaps a bartender or server will remember him. He has a good photo from the victim's LinkedIn profile to show around.

The paper and ink linked to the note found with the body have been identified. The brand isn't what he cataloged in the victim's home office, and the paper is sold at 14 stores within Detroit's city limits. Of course, in the age of Amazon, physical stores were the last place people shopped for stationery. Still, he would check it out. This and the bar from the night before are his only leads thus far.

Harlow grabs up his jacket, exits the station, and starts up his matte black Dodge Charger. Grand Rapids is just over a two-hour drive. It is well past noon, so the restaurant ought to be open. All the same, Harlow calls ahead. Someone knows something.

Chapter 12

Theresa tends to her backyard garden. Her father had created an impressive array of raised vegetable and herb gardens that capture most of the summer sun. Lining the yard are cedar hedges and additional gardens where nourishment for the bees and the butterflies are provided because of his efforts. A small pond with a fountain is something Theresa included a few years ago. She'd stocked it with goldfish, but the raccoons got to them the first year, and she couldn't bring herself to sacrifice any more.

The warmer weather is beginning to brighten Theresa's mood, as she enjoys nothing more than puttering around in her garden. A Japanese Maple, planted in 1969, offers a nice umbrella to the back corner of the yard where dandelions, white clover, and creeping Charlie have taken up residence. Weeds provide an opportunity to sit and let the repetition of pulling them place her in a meditative state. She would never dig them up outright or use chemicals to kill them. The practice of pulling them is a gift. Birds sing and visit the fountain to bathe and drink. The aroma of freshly cut grass and the feel of soil and dead leaves between her fingers complete the experience.

She breaths in deeply. Despite the white noise playing from her phone, she did not sleep well. This usually lulls her into a deep sleep, revitalizing her. Sleep is precious. It renews her body's defenses. It restores her energy where it is lost to her work. Peter's past life stuck with her. She tossed restlessly, trying to turn off her mind. She hopes not to revisit a long night after his next session.

Her phone rings, and she retrieves it from her pocket. It's her friend, Nyra.

"Hi there," she says, putting down her gardening utensil and standing.

"Hey, stranger! What's new?" Nyra is the opposite of Theresa in every way. Bubbly, married with children, stay-at-home-mom. She can't recall a single traumatic event that has interrupted her life. Kids thriving at school. A handsome husband. The best house in the 'hood, thickest lawn, nicest cars. If she didn't love her, she'd hate her.

"Oh, nothing to report," Theresa knows she sounds like a broken record, but she has never enjoyed talking on the phone. "Just doing some gardening."

"I love what a green thumb you have. Are you free tonight to go out for a drink?" If there's one thing Theresa doesn't envy in Nyra, it's her lack of free time. She would be a lousy friend to say no.

"Sure, I'm free after seven," it's like a reflex when Nyra asks to spend time with her. Still, some human contact outside of work does sound nice.

"Awesome, I'll pick you up at 7:30. There's this great new place downtown I'm hearing a lot about. We have to go!"

"Yes, sure, thank you, Nyra. I'll see you at 7:30." They say goodbye, and Theresa almost immediately suffers a low-level panic attack. Being out is problematic for her. She knows this about herself. Even after all the therapy and her education and career path, there's still a part of her who fears the outside world.

She breaths deeply again to ward off any more unpleasant feelings, hoping to embrace the moment. She won't be alone. Nyra knows enough to pick her up and take her to the destination. She won't leave her side. *Just breath.*

When 7:30 rolls around, Nyra is in the driveway, and Theresa is rushing out the door.

"You look nice," Nyra comments slyly as Theresa enters the vehicle. She is always hopeful Theresa will hook up with a guy when they go out. No thanks, she thinks.

"Thank you, you too," she's such a bad conversationalist. But Nyra knows this about her too. "How are the kids?"

"Oh, you know, *kids.* Mommy needs some time out," She turns out of the driveway before Theresa is even buckled in.

"And how are you doing?" Theresa continues to put the questions to Nyra to deflect her asking anymore.

Nyra sighs, "You know what, Tree?" That's her pet name for Theresa. She likes it. "I'm good. But I *need* this. We're going to have fun tonight." Her inner cheerleader announces while her grip on the steering wheel tightens.

Theresa laughs. "You seem animated tonight." That's saying something, too, as Nyra always seems animated, but tonight is different. *What's she hiding?*

"Truth be told, Tree, I'm a little restless." Her smile never fades, but her tone becomes more anxious. She's a heavier girl than Theresa but beautiful in that renaissance-painting way – wide hips and long hair. Maybe it's the bedroom eyes and the pouty lips. Her skin is the color of caramel and clear of any imperfections. She gets a lot of attention from men, and that's likely in no small part to her ample breasts. *Renaissance.* That is the perfect description for her. She belongs in one of those paintings.

"It must be hard being a mother to three kids under 7." Theresa surmises.

"Yeah," Nyra laughs out, "that's part of it." They turn onto the main drag, and Nyra eases down on the accelerator. Theresa has forgotten how nervous driving with her friend makes her feel.

"Is there more to it?"

"Save it for the bar. Do you want to get some appetizers? I left a casserole with the boys and Duke. I'm starting to feel a bit peckish now."

"I ate something but can always eat again," Theresa supports Nyra's need to escape the family for the night. A glass of wine will offer the required confidence to play this night out.

At the new establishment, Theresa chuckles over the name. "Oh, this has potential," she says, curious over the interior.

"Right? 'Quoth the Raven'? It's so charming." They move inside, and both stop to take it in.

It's beautiful, Theresa thinks. Low lighting sets the mood, ancient chandeliers with Edison lights. The beams and pillars are painted to match the spines of classic books. There are walls filled with books, or, at least, they appear to be books turned backward to reveal just their pages. A wrought-iron spiral staircase leads to nowhere. Bartenders with their groomed mustaches seem to have stepped out of some of these stories to serve you absinthe over sugar cubes.

"Welcome. Do you have a reservation?" A young woman dressed in black sporting a lacey, dark fascinator over her messy bun asks Nyra. People always focus on Nyra when the two go out. That cheerleader aura captivates any audience. The Hostess locates her name on the screen and leads them to a table built of old typewriters covered in a glass top. It is all very charming, Theresa thinks. They order a bottle of the house wine and continue to take it all in.

"Is that Patchouli I smell?" Nyra cranes her neck to see around the corner of the bar.

"Yes, with cinnamon, I think." Theresa is well versed in essential oils and has a nose for them. They smile at one another.

Nyra leans in, "didn't I tell you? This place already has my vote for new bar. Look at these menus!" Each menu displays a gothic imprint relatable to Poe's works, and the menu items themselves have relevant titles to describe them.

"It's so quaint," she agrees. "I had no idea." The wine arrives, and Nyra orders a small charcuterie board to start.

"You had no idea because you don't leave the house." Nyra lays a hand on her friend's. "I'm not judging, Tree, but I do worry. You know I worry." She picks up her glass and touches Theresa's with it. "Cheers!"

"Cheers," she says back, their glasses emitting a pleasant hum when they touch. Theresa imagines Nyra in her high school Cheer outfit, her high cheekbones lifting in that trademark, toothy grin. She tastes the wine. It's good. It's a dry Cab-Sauv. Gone are the days of the sweet wines. She can't stomach them anymore.

The women drain the bottle as the night progresses, and Theresa feels the artificial confidence kick in. Good, it's what she needs to be out like this.

"Peter?" Theresa says to the man walking past her table. He stops a moment, squinting in the low light, recognizing her. "Hi, how are you?"

Peter smiles and nods at Nyra also. "I'm good, thank you, how are you?"

"Good also. It's nice to see you." She can't expand on the conversation without mentioning his session, so she asks, "isn't this nice? Is this your first time here?"

"I actually came here a couple of nights ago for the first time. It's going to be my favorite place, I think." He laughs, knowing she knows where he works.

"Well, it was so nice bumping into you." She notices a mousey but attractive woman waiting for him at a distance and recognizes her too. She waves. "Is that - Clare?"

"Oh, yes, of course, you know Clare," he waves her over. She stands, and the two women hug for a moment.

"I'm so sorry, I didn't recognize you right away," Clare says. "You've taken on Peter as a client."

"Do I have you to thank for that?"

"I guess you do," Clare smiles up at Peter, and they kiss.

"Oh, you're a couple!" Theresa feels embarrassed but unsure why. Nyra waves at Clare and invites them to join their table.

"No, we don't want to be a bother, but it was nice seeing you. I'll see you next week!" Peter says in a buoyant tone she hadn't seen in him at his first session.

"You will," Theresa watches the new couple move off to the bar, where they have two tall, clear drinks waiting for them.

"Both are clients of yours?" Nyra is intrigued.

"Sorry I didn't introduce you; they are clients, yes. I can't discuss them, of course."

"Oh, that's okay. I just thought for a moment -"

"That he was an old boyfriend I'd never mentioned?"

"Well, you never mention anything like that to me. If you leave me to my own devices ..." She winks, and the mains arrive.

Theresa finds she's caught up watching the two at the bar, remembering Clare. She'd very nearly had her on a plane to take the same course she had years before. Peter looks happy. That gladdens her heart. He was approachable tonight without that sense of loneliness that accompanied him on their initial meeting. He has a girlfriend. How lovely.

"Oh, get out of your head, Tree," Nyra demands in the easy way she has about her. "You're staring!" She whispers.

Theresa snaps out of it and notices her child-sized pasta dish in front of her. "That's embarrassing." She says, her head down, studying the fettuccini. "Do you think they noticed?"

"No." Nyra spears her fork into the Cobb salad, which had *borne a thousand injuries to arrive on her plate*, the server had recounted. "You missed the clever descriptions given by the server as to how your dinner came to arrive, though."

"Oh," Theresa feels terrible for her friend. Is she being inattentive again? She tends to daydream. "I'm so sorry, Nyra, it won't happen again."

"Hey, it's *me*, Tree," she explains kindly. "Never mind, I just don't want you being called out on it by your clients." She winks and takes a bite of her salad.

Theresa feels her face strain to smile, consciously pushing the corners of her mouth up. Don't get too invested in your clients, she tells herself. It's unprofessional.

"So, what did he have to say about my fettuccini?" Theresa asks, wanting to get back on track.

"If you want to eat it, maybe I don't tell you," Nyra laughs. Theresa laughs along, spinning her fork in the noodles, lightly peppered with parsley.

With a small amount on her fork, Theresa looks about the restaurant and smiles. "This is a fascinating spot."

Nyra swallows and pats her napkin on her full lips. "We have to come again."

Theresa nods and chews her fettuccini thoughtfully.

Chapter 13

Peter looks over his shoulder at the two women enjoying their dinners. Detroit is a big place. It's odd he would run into his new therapist here. He knows three people. Clare, Sanderson, and Theresa. One of which he'd just as soon forget.

Clare reads through the menu and points out an appetizer they could share. Peter absently nods to the choice of calamari and takes a long sip of his drink. He scans a quote, one of many beautifully presented and cleverly placed throughout the restaurant, one of Poe's that reads: "*There is no exquisite beauty... without some strangeness in the proportion.*"

Peter meditates on the wisdom of these words and places himself squarely in the quote. His PTSD might qualify *his* strangeness. Then as quickly as the thought enters, it leaves in place of something cheerier as he considers adding framed prints of author quotes to the bookshop.

"So," Clare starts, waving a hand in front of his face to bring him back to the present, "I've seen your shop. Can I see your apartment tonight? I bet it's full of character like the store," she draws him in with her attentive gaze.

"Uh, sure, yes, absolutely. It's full of it." Peter realizes he was drifting and reestablishes a connection. "There's even a gargoyle below my front window. I don't know if you noticed it from the outside. It's a copy of the spitting gargoyle on the Notre Dame cathedral in Paris." She's amused by this. The idea she wants to see his apartment excites Peter. It's been years since he's enjoyed a woman's company.

"That's over the top," Clare sips from her paper straw. "What about the rest of the place?"

"Well, it's a two-bedroom, one bath, not updated or anything. Pretty sure they're the original taps and sinks. That means they'd be from the mid-1900s."

"Fascinating." He watches her lips seal around her straw. *Would she want to stay the night?* He feels slightly anxious over the idea but absolutely on board.

Clare leans on the bar with her elbow, resting her head on her hand. "So, I guess we should ask the burning question," she looks slyly at Peter, who swallows hard. "Who's your favorite author?"

Peter feels his shoulders relax and breaths deeply. "That's a tough one," he replies, stirring the straw in his gin & tonic. "I'm all over the place with genres. I don't stick to anything. If it interests me, I read it."

"So, let me rephrase the question," she says, looking into his eyes, "who's your favorite science fiction author?"

"Dan Simmons," he says without pause.

"The Hyperion novels got me into him," she says, and Peter nods.

"Me too, I have all four in hardcover, but I left them at my parent's place." Peter returns the question.

"I tend to stick to what I like," she answers. "Sci-fi is great, but – well, you know I love anything reincarnation, and reading Cloud Atlas in college put me on to David Mitchell. So, I've read all of his books."

"Loved his most recent," Peter agrees. Clare nods, having read it as well. Peter thinks it important she asked the question. They're both readers, and sharing their favorite authors is an intimate way to get to know one another.

Clare notices something or someone behind Peter, and he turns to look. "No! Don't look," she whispers/shouts. Peter turns back to her, his interest piqued.

"What is it?"

" *Who* is it," she clarifies. "He looks like a sailor or something." Peter leans in and says, "Like, in a past life?"

Clare nods, studying her mark, forefinger pushing up her glasses. She bites her bottom lip in thought. Peter is dying to turn and look.

"You're too good at this," Peter admits and begins to turn again. Clare grabs his arm to stop him. "Really?" Peter looks down at her hand, brows furrowed.

"Let me get through this first," Clare says. "Was Popeye based on a real person?"

Peter gives her a look of surprise. "Popeye the Sailor Man?!" He squeaks out.

"Shhh," she says giddily, her hand tightening around his forearm. He likes her playful touch. Clare continues to eye the stranger behind him.

"You have to let me look," he insists, shaking his head at her. She squeezes his arm again.

"Well, if there was a real Popeye, this guy was him." She releases her grip on him, and Peter takes this as his queue to discreetly follow her gaze.

Sure enough, the man's jutting chin and a blue t-shirt with a red collar match the comic book character decisively. He wears a worn baseball cap atop a furrowed brow with one eye narrowed, straining to see. "Jesus, where's his pipe?"

"Right?" Clare leans back, satisfied Peter sees it. "Now, where is Olive Oil?" They scan the bar, and Peter lands on a tall, lanky woman with a tight bun. She's an attractive woman, but Peter never saw Popeye's Olive Oil as such.

Peter nods toward the woman, and Clare finds her. "Can fictional characters get a second chance?" He asks.

Clare finishes her drink and puffs out her cheeks, her lips vibrating on the exhale. "I guess I'm reaching tonight." She admits, and then, surprisingly (or not), Popeye approaches Olive Oil, and the two kiss upon meeting.

Clare's mouth is agape. "No kidding," she says, dumbfounded.

"Unbelievable," Peter is at a loss as well. They turn to each other and smile brightly, giddy over their uncanny ability to pair people. Peter can't believe his luck in discovering Clare. They're eerily compatible, and he aches to be closer.

"That was easy," Clare says, and their appetizer arrives. They share the small portion of calamari, described as a *squid pulled from a chilling and dreary sea, cleaved to pieces, battered and fried, and presented as a dream within a dream.* They settle on waters to accompany the calamari, remarking comically on its appetizing description.

When the bill arrives, Peter insists he buys.

As they leave the bar, they wave at Theresa and her friend. In the car, Clare turns to him and leans in for a kiss. They stay parked for a time. Their tongues become entangled, and Peter experiences sensations reminiscent of his formative years with Ruby D'Angelo, his high school girlfriend. That didn't survive their stint in college, and after a couple of years of 'finding himself,' he joined the army and spent four years in active duty, wondering when he would be granted another moment like this. He is thrilled to be here again.

They drive away, and Clare's foot is heavier on the accelerator than when they drove to the restaurant. She's anxious to get back to his apartment. He's anxious over it too and wills her to go faster.

They enter the building, and she stops Peter in the shop to embrace him again. This kiss lingers, and he senses the evening's direction. He pulls away and asks if she'd like to see the apartment. She nods enthusiastically. He takes her hand and leads her up the stairs and past the living room into the bedroom.

"So, this is the bedroom," he says, and she pushes him onto the double bed; Peter twists to lay flat on his back; a stunned expression must show on his face as Clare crawls onto his lap. Her palms land on his chest, and she leans into him. They kiss each other in that sober way you kiss before things lead to the inevitable. Teeth touch, and lips spread apart, inviting tongues to mingle. A sense of urgency dominates, and Clare removes her top. He places his hands on her hips, one sliding up her slender stomach to her petite, firm breast. Peter allows Clare to pull off his shirt and then becomes entangled in it. They laugh at how chaotically they're navigating this moment, and Clare tugs harder at his sleeves, freeing his hands to return to her waist. Not long after, they are undressed, exploring each other's bodies.

Freeing a hand, he reaches for his bedside table, pulls open the drawer, and roots blindly around for his condoms. She helps him with it on. She moves in waves over his pelvis, taking control of the moment. Peter responds in kind, hips guiding his actions until a mutual gratification is reached. They play this out two more times throughout the night until they collapse next to one another in exhausted bliss.

Peter doesn't know what to say. His head is now trying to establish the proper response. Perhaps it's better to say nothing. Their actions spoke volumes. She runs her warm hand over his chest, beading with sweat, not unlike how she'd caressed the spine of the book he'd given her. He recalls sensing her touch at that moment. This was meant to be.

"I thought you wanted to see the gargoyle?" Always with the wit, he laughs at himself.

"Is that what we're calling it?" She reaches between his legs and rubs his engorged penis. She laughs at herself, burying her face into his hairless chest, their sweat mingling.

In the morning, she is up before Peter and showering. He takes this opportunity to satisfy a morning tradition and slips in next to her. The space is too small for both, making it easier to initiate his will. She is thrilled to see him, and they make love again under the warmth of the falling water.

Once dressed, she queries him about breakfast. "Do you have anything here, or would you like me to run out and pick something up while you open the shop?"

Peter feels embarrassed to admit he has nothing in the way of breakfast foods and suggests the bakery four doors down.

Once Peter has situated himself behind the store counter, Clare returns through the front door and hands Peter a chocolate croissant and a coffee. "I forgot to ask you what you take in it, so here are some creamers and sugars." She passes a small paper bag to him across the counter.

"This is perfect," Peter says, and not just about breakfast. "Are you free tonight?"

"I am," Clare replies excitedly. She's smitten, he thinks. Thank God it's not one-sided.

"Should we do this again? I mean, can you come back?"

"I can," she offers a stiff nod and that mischievous smile. His stomach does summersaults. He's captivated by her. She rounds the counter and lands another lingering kiss on him. He hadn't pegged her as so aggressive, but if last night is any indication... "Enjoy your breakfast. I'll pop in around 6:30? I'll bring dinner."

"Thank you," Peter says. "I'm looking forward to it." He suggests they exchange cell numbers, and she eagerly offers hers.

As she leaves, he studies her gait. She walks confidently, turning once she opens the door, blowing him a kiss. He returns the sentiment. She's incredible, he thinks.

Chapter 14

Harlow visits the location according to his bank statements that the victim last attended the night of his murder. It's a restaurant/bar in Grand Rapids downtown beside a swanky-looking hotel where he imagines business people congregate. It's on Monroe Center St NW, where the street is closed to vehicles. There are several bars and restaurants along this stretch. It's a vacation spot servicing traveling salespeople and families alike.

He finds the manager of The Little Bird and reminds her he's the detective who called earlier.

"Detective, Harlow," the older woman greets him. She wears a half dozen rings in her left ear and is graying at the temples. "I've called in all of our staff working that night for you to question." That was proactive of her, he thinks.

"Thank you," he says, and she motions for him to sit. "Were you also here that night?"

"Only until 10 pm," she explains. "The benefits of being the general manager." He nods at this.

"Then you had a night manager on? Could I speak with them first?"

She waves over a man in his mid-thirties dressed in a sports jacket and jeans. "This is Carson. He is my assistant manager and was here," she swallows. "He's compiled a spreadsheet for you of the transactions made that night."

"Thank you for that; very accommodating, Carson." Harlow enjoys the level of cooperation he's receiving.

"You're welcome," Carson says, a little stiff. Harlow gets this a lot – people tense up around authority. "I have forwarded it to your email as per Melissa's instructions." He looks at his manager.

"Excellent. Now, have you any suspicions remembering that night, where our victim is concerned?" Harlow knows Melissa has shown her staff the LinkedIn photo already.

"I'm afraid I can't say I noticed the man, sir. It was a busy night, as you'll see from our spreadsheet." Carson stands stock still, hands folded together across his pelvis.

Harlow reads him as telling the truth and asks several more questions of Carson. Nothing relevant is offered. He repeats his queries with the ten employees on duty that night, including kitchen staff. The bartender remembers the victim. He was obnoxious, she explains. He drank more than he should have and seemed to be on the prowl. She says this with a look of disgust, transforming her otherwise pleasant face. "He wanted to buy me a drink, but I refused." She looks at Melissa tentatively.

"I'm always being propositioned," Harlow can see why, as she is a beautiful twenty-something, but that doesn't make it right. "I never take them up on it, though. I'm not one of those girls."

"I'm sure," Harlow replies, "but as it stands, you *are* the last person who saw him alive." He studies her reaction. It's common for someone to feel intimidated by this statement, and she doesn't disappoint. "I'm not accusing you of anything, uh," he refers to her nametag, "Charlotte. It's just a fact, and I'd like to get as much information about his final hours as I can."

She nods and swallows hard. "I understand," she takes a breath. "He left at just about 1:30 am. You'll find he paid for his five drinks about 1:20."

"And did he leave alone?"

She nods again, "yes."

Harlow turns to Melissa, "do you have security footage you can offer me?"

"No, I'm sorry, we don't have security cameras. But the hotel next door does. You might like to ask them."

Harlow thanks Melissa and her staff for their time and lets Charlotte know he will be in touch if he thinks of any other questions.

The hotel manager of the City Flats hotel offers his footage of the night to assist in any way he can. A very open group, Harlow thinks. It's rarely this easy. The security footage reveals an interesting interaction with a couple at 1:37 am, and he has the manager move the data onto his team for forensic analysis. Perhaps between the home and hotel footage, something will turn up.

It sounds like the wife of his victim had more to worry about than just an absentee husband and father. As Charlotte suggested, if he was on the prowl, then perhaps there is a scorned lover out there with a motive.

That night, Harlow returns to the victim's home to walk the perimeter in the dark. This way, he gains firsthand experience of where a perp would need to move to avoid detection from the home security cameras and floodlights.

He finds a loophole in the security at the garage side of the house. He waves his hands at the motion light, but the lights do not come on. He knows this side of the house is blind to the cameras. He tries the side entrance into the garage and finds it's unlocked. *Curious.* Once inside the garage, he discovers the door leading into the house is locked. Was the victim shameless enough to have relations in the garage below where his wife and child were sleeping? Harlow seems to be building a case that tells a story of the victim having an affair, or at least thought he was about to.

So, who hated him so much as to murder him, frame it as a suicide, and leave a note? Not many people would go to so much trouble. It must be someone he was close to. Someone he'd wronged. The evidence, though, isn't supporting the violence. Not yet, at least.

The victim's car is with the forensics unit and will have been checked for hair and fiber, but there's no reason to believe the perp came back to the house in his car. The neighbors hadn't mentioned an unfamiliar car on the street that night. So, he will wait for the full forensics report before stirring up too many scenarios.

Harlow returns home and undresses. He carries a scar on his shoulder where a perp had thrust a knife into him years earlier. Beyond that and the lines in his furrowed brow, his career hasn't taken a terrible toll on his body.

Sitting on his second-hand, black leather couch, he pushes the whiskey bottle aside, a prominent feature on his coffee table. Not tonight, he tells himself. He places his files on the table to review. The folder is getting thicker with all the interviews. He pulls out the most recent with the bartender from the restaurant. Charlotte seemed a bit put off over the whole exercise, but Harlow doesn't suspect her of foul play. She'd said his victim was on the prowl. That sticks with Harlow. It offers an opportunity for the victim to be lured into a false sense of security. He was drunk. He was looking.

Harlow leans back, and his ex-wife assaults his memories. She, too, was beautiful. He often wondered how he'd done so well. She never liked his line of work. But she married him anyway. Harlow stares at the bottle, half-empty; nothing was ever half full to him. Tiff had left him because of that. That's what she'd told him. She didn't appreciate his dark side. When it ended, that's all he had.

He picks up the lighter and ignites the flame. Staring at it flickering in the low light inspires him to run it under his forearm. The pain is real when it leaves a mark he can see. It makes the memories he's plagued with real. It offers pain where he feels nothing anymore.

A frown pulls down the landscape of his hardened face as the pain reassures him his past had happened and that his present is the result.

Chapter 15

The weekend spent with Clare was bliss. Peter wore a smile most of the time. The bookstore saw steady business as summer reading lists were being bought up at an accelerated rate.

The weekdays seemed to melt together until his next session with Theresa was on top of him. Tonight, he will not see Clare as she's spending the evening with her fellow employees at a team-building event a hundred miles east of the city. He is becoming increasingly fond of her and catches himself imagining the next time they meet. They've texted throughout the day, and he receives one now stating how she sees their next encounter playing out.

Is this sexting? He asks himself. *Do I sext back?* He feels awkward over the notion but finds himself responding in kind. He visualizes Clare's body and discovers he's becoming aroused. Not a great position to be in with three people currently browsing the bookstore. He's thankful for the counter.

A middle-aged man approaches and lays three books down. A trilogy of the Sci-fi genre. It's excellent, Peter recalls and tells the man so.

"I've read another trilogy from the author and found it enlightening," the tall, lanky man replies.

"I love it when a novel or series offers more than just a story," Peter admits. "If I can walk away from a book with a new idea to ponder, I feel like I've paid for more than mere entertainment."

"Exactly," the man says, his eyes wandering about the store. "Do you have a book club running out of your shop?"

A great idea that Peter had once suggested to Sanderson but was shot down. The man didn't have a clue about how to market a business like this. Sanderson told him the store belongs to an ex-wife who lives abroad and that it is in her name, and she has an accountant send her the profits quarterly. Of course, Sanderson skims heavily before handing anything over to the accountant. He was proud to make that announcement.

Still, Sanderson has multiple businesses well outside the scope of publishing and rare book sales but has no penchant for marketing. Peter thinks it is a wonder he's done as well as he has.

"It's an idea I'd love to implement," Peter explains to the man, "but the boss has other ideas."

"You have a perfect sitting area, and a group could meet once a week to make it viable. You would order the books as they are announced and gain profits from the sales."

"As I said, a great idea," Peter considers the request and screws up his face. "Why not? The boss isn't here; let's plan it. Are you with a club now you'd like to move here?"

"I would love that. The library is fine, but they close so early. I'm Ted, by the way."

Peter feels that sense of kismet again and makes the call. "Peter. Here's my number. Let's shoot for next week."

"We've just finished a book, so that would be perfect. I'll recommend this trilogy and let you know. We have been meeting on Thursdays. Would Thursday work for you?"

"It does. The store closes at 6. I could let everyone in at 7. I have more folding chairs in the back room."

"Perfect. I'll let you know the details. We're roughly six readers at this time."

"Then we'll have enough seating."

"Can we bring in a fruit tray and wine?"

"Absolutely." That the idea is taking form excites Peter.

"Is it possible to start tomorrow?" Ted pushes. "I can make the arrangements." Ted becomes more animated as the conversation becomes a plan.

"Why not?" Clare will likely enjoy the experience too. "I'll see you at 7."

Ted completes his cash payment, and Peter feels a warmth envelop him. This is good. This is what he had hoped might happen under his management; like-minded people meeting to discuss books.

At 5:30, he closes and makes his way to Theresa's for his regression therapy.

Once at the house, they chat briefly over their unlikely meeting at 'Quoth the Raven' and Clare's enthusiasm over past life regression. Peter explains that the last week has been one good turn after another, and he can see that Theresa is genuinely happy for him.

"When you seek help the way you've done, often you'll experience positive benefits immediately," Theresa says openly. "The universe is listening."

In the session room, he relaxes in the chaise lounge, whereas the time before, he felt a little awkward lying on someone else's chaise with a blanket drawn over him. This time he feels empowered. Had he the past life regression to thank for so many positive results? Whatever it is, he fancies himself a believer now. Still, he is anxious about reliving another life or two that could cause him more emotional upheaval. But he puts the thought out of his mind deciding what will be will be and that it is for the good of his present.

In Theresa's care, Peter finds that perfect balance of energy and drifts into a state of hypnosis. It's a curious sensation to be alert to the present while moving through a corridor in his mind's eye.

He chooses a door. It is a grand doorway with a half-circle above it; intricate carvings adorn the heavy wood, and Peter pushes the double door inward with a thought. He explains the scene as he witnesses it in the first person. A sense of foreboding enters his chest. *Where are the happy moments? Why is all he's experiencing cruel and final ones?*

And so, this life too shows the same indications of a final, terrifying moment in a life he places in France during what is coined: *The Terror.*

Peter rapidly explains to Theresa that he witnesses masses of people gathered in an ancient plaza, around a central stage where there stands a guillotine. The sky is bright blue with not a cloud in it. Gulls fly overhead. He smells bonfires and fear. The crowd cheers. There are others, like him, who form a line. Heads will roll today, and his will be among them.

Panic enters, and Peter feels a knot form in his stomach as he takes the wooden stairs up to the raised platform. His breathing is labored. His executioner is a man without rank. A commoner. He asks Peter if he has any final words. Peter can't talk, his throat constricts, and his tongue fails him.

"Look into his eyes, Peter," Theresa urges him as she had with the first one.

Peter struggles to see the executioner's face. Then he lands on the man's eyes. They are wide open and hungry for blood, justice, or whatever it is he thinks he will accomplish through Peter's death. The crowd cheers on the man and those holding the other victims in place.

Peter is asked to bend the knee and refuses. He is forced down, and his head placed past the bottom half of the lunette where his neck is meant to rest. The top portion is lowered quickly and secured.

Peter feels restless and anxious over his end. Theresa asks him to recognize his executioner. He revisits the man's alert gaze of a moment earlier and identifies a current set of eyes staring back.

The guillotine is released, and Peter can hear it cutting the air above him until it severs his head from his body. He feels nothing but is entirely aware his head is now detached. He blinks once, twice, and then Theresa snaps him out of the traumatic episode.

"You're here, with me, in the present. You're safe, Peter. Appreciate the message the past is giving you. It's part of you, and remembering it can heal."

He shakes his head at the memory, fingers caressing his throat. "Why am I dying in my past lives?"

"It's another link to your PTSD," she surmises. "Your pasts are giving you examples of what trauma looks like."

"But I know what trauma is. I already suffer it." He's confused by his unconscious choices in choosing doors to lives that have ended in cruel and unusual deaths.

"We need to look at the obvious signs. Your experiences are showing you those responsible for your untimely deaths."

"This one was recent," Peter says, still foggy from the hypnosis. He tries to sit upright but is too weak to push himself up from the lounge. "Are these not doing more to agitate my PTSD?"

"I believe it is a way to help you cope," Theresa suggests. "Not to downplay your current issues, but rather to show you who to avoid in the present."

"Right, so what's the lesson? Identify my tormentors and walk away from everything? From my life?" Peter is frustrated.

Theresa smiles empathetically, her head tilting slightly to the right. "To live in the present. You've decided to stay at the bookstore despite your difficult boss. You're not in imminent danger of dying. You're healthy. You've met a girl. You have a job and a place to live. You can overcome your past to live in the now. That includes your recent past."

Peter nods, knowing he has made significant strides in his life with Clare and the bookstore. That he will begin a book club tomorrow night is something he's always hoped to accomplish.

"That's fair," he admits, now able to push himself to a seated position. "You know, I'm starting a book club at the shop tomorrow night."

"That sounds wonderful," Theresa says, "and did you recognize your executioner?" She wants to get back to the work.

He did. He feels at odds with what he witnessed, though. He's strangely confident the very man who has arranged the book club meetings was the one who took his head during the Reign of Terror in revolutionary France. He explains this discovery and his executioner's current manifestation.

"That's curious that he's now come back to offer assistance in your life," but Theresa doesn't look convinced; Peter notices. "I would be wary of him, though, Peter. Be cautious in your dealings with this man."

Peter feels uneasy over her warning. "Can a man not return to your life in a different role? A helpful one?"

"Not a common occurrence in my experience. Look at your boss; was it Sanderson? Has he been a good influence on your life?"

Peter looks at Theresa and shakes his head. "He's supplied me with a job and housing, but he's a bully, an *asshole*."

"And a trigger for your PTSD."

"Yes," Peter sees where she's going with this.

"He may have come into your life merely to torment you," she reminds him. "He has situated himself in a power position over you and, as you said, is an asshole." She smiles sympathetically.

Peter shakes his head again. "He's not around much."

"And that makes you happy."

"Better he's not micromanaging my every move." Peter isn't missing him.

"Okay, then. Let's consider this new influence who took your head. Does this new information cause you pause to allow him access into your life?"

"I don't know. I mean, it's just a book club. There will be people there," Peter notices Theresa lean in, resting her elbows on her thighs. He senses she might like an invite. "Did you want to come? 7 pm. The Bookaneer on East Warren Ave. They'll be reading A.I. Insurrection; it's the first in a completed trilogy."

"Science fiction? Not really my genre," she leans back again, "but I appreciate the offer."

"I'll feel him out," Peter suggests. "Sanderson, I get, but this guy seems harmless."

"You'll let me know next week when we meet again. For now, tread carefully and continue using the tools you have when you begin to feel anxious." Theresa stands. "Write down the events and people who cause you stress."

"I will, but, no offense, how will I know if all of this is helping?" Peter's hands move in circles to encompass the room with all its crystals and candles and comfortable seating. He feels like nothing is being accomplished outside of identifying past life traumas.

"It's a process, Peter. Give it time. The more you learn about your past, the better you'll be suited to face the present and all of its triggers."

Peter considers what she's saying and realizes he's slept better the past week. No nightmares he can remember. That could be on account of Clare coming into his life, but it could be that he's releasing the past through this practice. If nothing else, it's incredibly thought-provoking.

"I'd like to focus on your throat chakra, Peter," Theresa suggests. "It's been weakened by your tragic deaths and requires attention."

"My - chakra?"

"Yes, here is a pamphlet on stretches you can do on your own. The information inside will give you other options as well." She hands him the piece of paper. "Wear blue as often as possible until I see you next week and can assess again. Blue is the color attached to your throat chakra."

"A blue collared shirt?" Peter asks, and Theresa nods. "I can do that."

Peter leaves her house and boards the bus back to his apartment. He wants to speak with Clare. He wants to hear her thoughts on how regression therapy will help him cope. He pulls his phone out of his pocket and thinks better of it. She's at a retreat for work. He doesn't want to be that guy, even though he knows he is.

They'll discuss it tomorrow when he sees her.

Chapter 16

Peter slept lightly last night, waking up three times. It took a few minutes to get out of his head on each occasion and fall back to sleep, so he's feeling fatigued. Did he dream? He thinks he did, but nothing surfaces.

The bookstore has a busy day with people popping in to find something they can take on holiday up to the cottage or some other remote retreat. He envies those with the option.

He reads through the pamphlet Theresa had given him, conscious of the color of the shirt that he slipped on after his shower. The throat chakra is responsible for timidness and making sound decisions. Apparently, his chakra is blocked. After being lynched and having his head severed, it makes a lot of sense to Peter.

When the store closes, he receives a phone call from Ted, the man coming with his book club in an hour. Peter assures him the space is ready, and he'll open the door to everyone when they arrive. He has a few extra copies of the first book in the series they'll start, but Ted says they'll likely just discuss their last book and get a feel for the place.

When he puts the phone down, there is a rapping at the door, and he finds Clare smiling and waving in the rain. Peter dashes to the door and opens it, taking her spring coat and hanging it on a hook.

"Can no one predict the weather anymore?" Clare asks, removing her glasses and rubbing the rain-speckled lenses on her dry shirt.

"Climate change," Peter states, locking the heavy, glass door. Clare nods, and they kiss. While engrossed in Clare's warmth,, part of Peter wishes he hadn't planned the book club for tonight. Right now, he'd much rather spend the rest of the evening with just her.

"So, you'd mentioned in your text that the team building went well," Peter wants to hear more.

"It did," she replies, her lenses now fogging over. "We did the usual, you know, trust falls, blindfold direction, etcetera. It was good. We had some laughs."

"Happy to hear it." She seems uninterested in talking about yesterday, and Peter gets the message. "So, the book club will be in an hour."

"Oh, I forgot our dinners in the car!" She turns to go back out into the rain, and Peter volunteers before she can protest, taking her purse.

"I'm just right out front," she giggles, and he's back in a flash with the burritos.

Peter locks the door and looks at the packaging, unconsciously making a face. "You might be accelerating the 'get to know me' phase with this meal." He loves Mexican food, but it doesn't always love him back.

Clare gets the insinuation and shrugs it off. "They're the best in the city," she assures him, accompanied by her trademark nod. They sit at the counter to eat, and when they've finished their foot-long burritos, Clare excuses herself, taking her overnight bag up to his apartment. She's left half her meal, and Peter wraps it and places it in the office mini-fridge.

Moments later, there is a new knock on the door, and Peter sees that it's Ted. The rain seems to have paused. Peter sees no one with him, so Theresa's warning activates a gut decision. He fiddles with the lock and asks through the glass where the rest of his group is.

"I'm early so I can greet them when they arrive." It's not seven yet, and Peter notices the clock over his shoulder. Still, he continues to fuss with the lock. He takes this time to assess all Ted has brought with him. A bookish-looking leather satchel over his shoulder, a heavier than necessary trench coat, and a bottle of something in a brown paper bag. It all looks harmless enough, but he can't get Theresa's warning out of his head.

"I'm so sorry, this lock sticks sometimes," Peter apologizes, still searching his feelings over allowing the lanky stranger in. There is accompanying anxiety deep in his gut that ignites when he locks eyes on Ted. The same eyes that forced him onto the guillotine. It's an uncomfortable sensation and one he tries to swallow. "At least the rain's tapered off."

To stall Ted another few minutes until the rest of the club arrives, he suggests he will fetch a tool from the back to force the lock. Ted looks agitated by this. But then, who wouldn't be. It isn't exactly the nicest night.

Peter pretends to look for the elusive tool in the office and watches the digital clock on the desk. 6:58 pm. Two more minutes. Make it five, he thinks. At 7:03, he pulls a wrench from one of the drawers and hurries back to the front door. Ted is looking less and less amused. Peter bangs at the top latch as if loosening it.

"No one yet?" Peter stares past Ted.

"No one yet," Ted replies coolly. "New location. I'm sure they'll be here soon. They often carpool."

Peter isn't sure he's buying it, but he's not making a great impression on a potentially good customer if it's 'true.' Still, the sense something is wrong compels him to carry on the façade. "This isn't doing it. I'm so sorry. I was looking for the hammer, not a wrench." He goes back to the office.

He hears the bell above the door clang a moment later and feels suddenly vulnerable. Then Clare's voice rings out.

"You must be Ted," she's saying to him. *Christ, she's come down and seen him and unlocked the door.* Peter will look like a damn fool now. He pops out of the office.

"Are you kidding me?" He says comically. "I must have loosened it for you."

Ted is unimpressed but smiles down at Clare, handing her the bottle of wine. "Thank you. Yes, I'm Ted, and you are?"

Clare introduces herself and unbags the bottle. "Oh, I like this one!" She places it on the counter, and Peter forces himself to shake Ted's hand.

"Do you think they have the right address?"

"No, but I do," Ted pulls a small pistol on Peter and shouts for both to lay on the floor with their hands joined over their heads.

Goddamn it, Peter thinks, go with your gut. But it was Clare who'd let him in. Clare, oh god, she'll be terrified. Peter understands guns. He could effectively pull Teds apart and rebuild it in under a minute, but Ted got the jump on him, and now he's on his knees, slowly lowering himself to his stomach. He looks back at Clare, who is doing the same.

"Take what you want; just let us be," Peter tells Ted a little shakily. "We're cooperating," He feels the adrenaline rush but must quash it. He's sweating, and his blood pressure is through the roof. Anxiety is taking a back seat right now. Peter's senses heighten, his focus narrows, and he scrutinizes Ted's movements through narrowing vision as the robber shuffles around the store wildly. Peter catches subtle sounds – a sniff here, a scratching there. Ted is wired. Peter's fists clench, and his muscles constrict, ready to leap into action. If Clare weren't in the room, he would put these enhanced senses, and his military training to good use, but he can't risk Clare. He won't.

"Where's the safe?" Ted orders. Peter looks up at him and sees that the man is vibrating. He's tense. Peter just points to the counter. "Show me!"

Peter rises slowly, hands linked behind his head. "It's this way." Ted follows. Peter nods at the wall safe, and Ted orders Peter to open it. Ted fills his empty bag with the cash and the rare books.

"You stay down," Ted warns Clare, who is still in his line of sight. "You, open the register." He nudges Peter with the barrel of the gun, and Peter does as he's instructed, all the while considering and reconsidering scenarios where he overpowers Ted. There isn't much in the register, but he hands it over.

Ted, probably not his real name, my executioner, Peter thinks. *Will he repeat his crime and shoot me now?* The adrenaline which had sparked Peter's fight response now betrays him as anxiety rushes in. Peter's breathing is shallow, and he feels faint. Not much of an impression he'll be leaving with Clare. But if they come out of this unharmed, he'll take it as a win.

"What else have you got in here worth anything?"

"Just our lives," Peter replies. "You've taken everything."

Ted orders Peter back on the ground, and he lands next to Clare. Their elbows touch, and in a whisper, he tells her that it will be okay. Clare nods and squeaks something.

Ted is heard shuffling from shelf to shelf, stuffing books into his satchel. The son of a bitch is robbing him blind. "Purse," he tells Clare. She lifts her arm, and he pulls it away, emptying its contents. He takes her wallet and then demands Peter's.

"In my front pocket," Peter rolls to his side so Ted can reach it. He pockets it as well. Ted seems to be loitering now. He has everything. Peter's anxiety is through the roof. If he could access his training without worry, he would, not for the bookstore but for himself. This is a humiliating experience. *It's going to fuck everything up.* He's doing the work to be better, and then this happens. And what about Clare? Will she ever want to come here again? The scene of this nightmare? Will she want to see him again? Him, who did nothing to stop this? She'll associate this with Peter now. The thought is unbearable.

Peter sizes up Ted's position and develops a plan. "When he goes behind the bookshelf again, run upstairs," he explains calmly to Clare. She shakes her head. "Please, I can stop this, but not with you in the room."

"I won't let you risk your life," she whispers back. "Peter. Please. Don't." He considers her plea presented through tears. If she doesn't do as he asks, he can't go on the offensive with Ted. He won't. He realizes that the son of a bitch was just scoping out the store yesterday, thinking back on Ted's wandering eyes.

Ted mutters something, and the bell over the door rings. Peter looks up and realizes Ted has left. He feels slightly emasculated but scrambles up to his feet and watches through the picture window as the thief runs up the street in what is now a driving rain. He's lost his chance. Peter locks the door and returns to Clare, who has now assumed the fetal position on the floor.

He kneels to comfort her. She hugs him hard and won't let go. Ted left the car keys and the car. Maybe he couldn't drive. He never demanded or took their cell phones. Peter holds his and dials 911, still embracing Clare as she sobs into his shoulder.

Chapter 17

Ted, or as he's known to his friends, *Zach*, sits in his basement apartment in the early morning hours after he'd robbed The Bookaneer and fallen asleep. He's questioning his actions now, though the plan went off without a hitch. A medium-sized figure dressed in black and wearing a balaclava paces his cracked, tile floors. He can't decern whether it is a man or a woman. Dressed in baggy clothes, a heavy jacket, maybe sweatpants, and non-descript black boots, they had appeared from nowhere. He has a head injury and aches to feel for the bump and soothe it with his hand. As his vision steadies and consciousness returns, he groans. The last thing he remembers is laying on top of his sheets and drifting.

The figure is unsympathetic. They continue to pace. Something is in their left hand. He can't make out what the object is. Zach begs the shadowy figure not to hurt him further, realizing he is bound to his kitchen chair. He's helpless, like the two he'd left on the bookstore floor. He wriggles a little to see if the ropes have any give. They don't. He's bent over with his wrists tied to the wood spindles of the chair.

Still, the figure paces about his flat. He thinks fleetingly that they may be reconsidering their next move. A hand grabs his hair and snaps his head back. He looks into his captor's eyes and pleadingly asks for forgiveness. What he receives is cold indifference. The hidden head tilts to the left, saying nothing. *What sort of bookstore had connections like this?* Was this even linked to his recent robbery? He has more enemies than friends.

A card is presented, and he thinks the design is quite clever. He reads the words carefully. This robs him of any hope. It terrifies him. Zach begins to struggle violently with the ropes now, realizing he has no other option but to try to escape. The figure still has a tight hold of his hair, and it hurts to pull against it.

After a short time, he relents. He hasn't the strength to pull free from his bonds, and his head screams against the effort. He's finished.

Chapter 18

Peter puts Clare to bed once the police have left with their report. He's wired, whereas Clare is exhausted. He lets her sleep and decides to take a long walk, having locked the door and checked it three times. The rain has subsided, and the night is humid. He needs to walk off the adrenaline. He runs through scenarios where he might have disarmed the thief, but returns to his original conclusion, that the gun may have gone off and struck Clare.

He shakes his arms out at his sides as the anxiety of the event continues to play on his nervous system. More of the same, he thinks. PTSD. He hasn't had a gun pulled on him since he was in the service, and that was just during training exercises. This was real life, and he feared he'd frozen. Fight or flight and all that. Is this who he is? Is he the type that takes flight? Not exactly; he'd calmly done what the thief had asked. He hadn't fled. But he hadn't fought either. Jesus, he thinks, this will haunt me.

The police told them they'd done everything exactly right. Maybe *that* was his training? He can't remember. His mind is racing. The more he considers what he'd done and what the police had explained, the less anxious he feels over his actions. He'd assessed the situation and acted accordingly. No one was hurt save his pride and Clare's mental health. He may yet pull out of this encounter without further emotional damage.

Peter's thoughts move to Theresa next. She had warned him against inviting this man into his life, and his gut told him not to open that door. Clare had surprised him, letting Ted in like that. This could have been avoided.

Sanderson's ex-wife would hear about the robbery, he surmises. It's her store. He's never met the woman, but he imagines she's not a tyrant after divorcing Sanderson.

A shadow slips into the cover of an alleyway, and Peter once again feels the familiar surge of adrenaline. It's after one in the morning. It's stupid to be out like this right now. The streets are mostly dead. There is a single bar emptying. He moves past a straggler walking home, witnesses a cab pull away from the sidewalk, and studies a pair of eyes staring blankly from a passing bus. His pace quickens.

Peter decides to cross the street, avoiding the alley. Should he turn back now? The adrenaline wasn't easing off nearly fast enough, and exercise is what Peter finds works best. If he doesn't burn it off, he'll never sleep. But being out was beginning to feel wrong. Next, a tall man with wild hair exits a 24-hour pawn shop just two shops ahead of him. Peter feels a wave of recognition wash over him. The man is tall and skinny. Paired with his gait, Peter thinks of Ted. His palms sweat, and his eyesight narrows, focusing on the man. He'll follow him, he decides. If it's Ted, what will he say? Rather, what will he do? Had he just pawned the stolen books? It had been hours since he'd robbed the store. Still, Peter feels empowered by the rush of possibilities and keeps on him.

The man turns, and Peter flinches at his profile. He descends a cement staircase, and Peter gulps in the humid air of the city.

Chapter 19

"The body was found by the woman being questioned," the constable points out the thin, dirty blonde scratching at track marks along the inside of her left forearm. "Some help she's going to be."

Harlow nods and sizes up the scene. He usually wouldn't work this end of his city, but his captain explained the situation. Harlow's gaze lands on the card. It's identical to the one found on the businessman's body. He picks it up, already bagged, and reads the inscription. Same ominous statement. It will be an interesting task linking the two cases, he thinks. This guy is known to the 5th precinct as a small-time criminal. Theft, mostly. Some dealing. The girl answering questions is a likely client.

"I ain't seen no one," the woman tells the officer. "I got a key, and Zach – he lets me sleep here sometimes," her face contorts as she glances at the body. "I called 'cause I found him," her skeletal arm flies from her side.

Harlow notices she's skittish, expecting a hit, when instead she gets this mess. Foot tapping and scratching her self-inflicted wounds, her eyes survey the squalid basement apartment. She's wondering where Zach stashes the drugs her body aches for, he thinks. There's no blood spatter on her crop top, but Harlow isn't considering her for the murder. The note is enough to take her out of the equation. Still, he'll have her confirm her whereabouts the night of the other murder.

The FBI will be even more embedded in his case now. This is unquestionably the work of a serial killer. Harlow can hardly believe he's now the lead investigator on a case of this magnitude. When will they tell the public? Will they tell them? At this point, he sees no apparent connection to the two murders save the note. They certainly live in different worlds. Both victims were killed in unusual but very different ways. Next, he takes a closer look at the victim.

The death is far grizzlier than the first. He imagines hacking a man's head off is something one really has to commit to in the moment. Harlow's never seen anything like it. The blood pooled around the body is thick, as is its scent. The murder is timed at about six hours old. The arterial spray hit the ceiling and the wall in front of the victim. Harlow marvels over the sheer force of will of a heart to beat without purpose. Just a pump moving the blood until it empties into the room. He looks next for a silhouette on the wall where the murderer might have stood - nothing of consequence. Forensics is on the scene. They say the note sat on the victim's severed head; the head was placed on the deceased's lap under his hands as if left to hold it in place. Harlow finds this profoundly unsettling.

Serial murderers can become detached from their crimes. They dehumanize the victim to satisfy some abnormal psychological gratification. Taking a man's head like this – Harlow can't imagine it being an easy task. The killer would have had to chop their way through muscle and bone and endured blood spatter. The stump sitting over the body's shoulders is a grizzly mess, the victim's shirt drenched in the sticky gore. He suppresses a bout of laughter, pushing it into his chest, seeing the scene as comical in all its ghoulish glory. Harlow takes another walk around the basement, fighting the urge to laugh aloud. A look at the door reveals no forced entry. Not unlike what Harlow suspects of the first murder, maybe Zach had let his attacker in? *Or had they waited in the shadows? Why? How are these two murders linked?*

Harlow's phone rings, and he places it to his ear. "Harlow," he says like he's clearing his throat.

"Detective, this is Detective Costain of the Robbery-Homicide 10th division; I believe your victim is linked to an armed robbery we responded to last night."

Harlow remembers Costain; she's shown impressive results in her recent promotion and is making a name for herself. "Is that so?"

"Yes, I saw the preliminary report of your murder case, and our witness description of their thief is dead on." She pauses. "Zach Denisov is a career criminal who has been arrested multiple times on theft under $5000 and been in the system for dealing three times."

"Okay," Harlow isn't sure how the preliminary report made it to her eyes, but if it moves his case along, this could be the break he's looking for. "That's welcome information, detective. I'd like to speak to your witnesses."

"Of course, I will have them come in tonight for you to question."

"Thank you, let me know when and where," Harlow wouldn't be in the Cornerstone Village district of Detroit if it weren't for the link the first murder shares with this one.

"5th Precinct, 6 pm." She hangs up, and Harlow pockets his phone.

After connecting the identity of his victim to the robber, at 6 pm, he's waiting on the witnesses of the armed robbery to arrive in the small interrogation room provided to him at the 5th precinct. The door opens, and Harlow stands to greet his guests. Costain, a tall woman with a raspy voice and short, dark hair, enters first. She shakes Harlow's hand with a firm, one thrust pump and directs the two witnesses to their chairs.

"This is Detective Harlow," Costain introduces them, "he is the lead investigator on the murder of your thief."

"Peter," the young man introduces himself. "Clare," the pretty, slight woman says. Both look nervous. Neither looks to Harlow like they might have committed a crime that left a man beheaded, but he will grill them regardless.

"Thank you for coming in on such short notice," Harlow begins and slides their wallets and other assorted possessions found at the scene toward them. "It seems the man who robbed you last night was murdered six or seven hours after fleeing your shop." He stops to assess their reaction. Their stunned expressions look genuine. They take each other's hands.

"After you'd sat with the police and gave your report of the theft, what did you do next?" Harlow is keeping it as conversational as possible so as not to make them feel like they are being considered for the murder. "I'm just trying to place everyone. Did you see him again during the night? Did he return?"

The woman, Clare, speaks up. "We went to bed almost immediately after Detective Costain left," she explains, looking back at Peter. She's telling the truth; Harlow is sure of it. His focus moves to Peter, who nods along. "We were exhausted after the ordeal," she continues.

"Understandable," Harlow replies. "Then you had no further dealings with this man?"

Peter shakes his head. "Like we told Detective Costain, he had fooled us into thinking we were starting a book club."

"And he used that angle to gain after-hours entry," Harlow nods, "and you had no prior relationship with this man?"

"None," Peter assures him, and he is buying it. "We thought his name was Ted."

"So, you both fell asleep and didn't wake again until morning?" He's convinced of Clare's story but questions Peter's.

"Well, I couldn't sleep right away and went for a walk to burn off the anxiety," Peter admits, "I have PTSD from Afghanistan, and last night didn't do anything to help that."

Harlow raises an eyebrow at this. Peter is a Vet and understands violence. He went for a walk the same night Zach was killed just blocks from his apartment.

"In fact," Peter has more to tell him, "I thought I'd seen Ted – uh, Zach walking in front of me at one point, but then when the man turned to look my way, I saw that it wasn't him."

"Thank you," Harlow says, "what time was that, do you think?"

"Maybe 1 am?"

"And you turned around to go home from where? Do you remember?"

"Yes, at a pawn shop, near Van Dyke." Harlow watches as Peter considers his story.

"And you returned home when?" Harlow will time himself from Van Dyke to The Bookaneer to ensure Peter's timeline adds up. He'll also canvass the street for surveillance footage that aligns with the times Peter is offering.

"I guess about 1:15?" Peter seems unsure of his answer. "It was a bad night; I'm sorry if my memory isn't perfect. We'd been through a lot." He looks at Clare, and Harlow notices him squeezing her hand. She squeezes back and places her other hand on top of his.

"Thank you for coming in; we're grateful for your assistance in piecing the night together." Harlow stands. "I may call on you at your shop if I think of anything else."

Peter and Clare nod, and Costain leads them out, directing them to the front doors. She returns to Harlow. "What do you make of that confession?"

"Was that a confession?" Harlow asks, his thumbs typing out commands to have East Warren Avenue from Outer Dr. East and Cadieux canvassed for video surveillance.

"I don't mean to say he'd just admitted to the murder, but he didn't hold back."

"It was very forthcoming, but he could just be getting ahead of any suspicions when we poll for video footage from last night," Harlow slips his phone back into his front pocket.

"He's guessed you'll be looking for things like that and doesn't want to be ID'd without being upfront about his walk." Costain nods.

"Clever," Harlow says of Peter's quick thinking. "But who wants to be wrongly accused of something like this?"

"Is he a suspect then?"

Harlow tilts his head until a satisfying crack emits from his neck, closes his eyes a moment, and takes a deep breath. "Innocent until proven guilty." He would have to link Peter to the first murder somehow to accuse him of Zachdon't's. And the first murder seems unrelated on every level.

Chapter 20

Theresa sits with her friend at her kitchen island as they sip on a local Pinot Gris. Theresa is grateful to have her friend join her this afternoon as the rain washes away any thoughts of stepping outside.

"Not exactly the summer they promised," Nyra looks sad. It must be difficult for a mother with young children unable to enjoy the outdoors. Nyra takes a long sip of the wine.

"I can't remember the last time a forecast was right," Theresa places a small live-edge wood board down on the counter with assorted meats, cheeses, nuts, and vegetables adorning it.

Nyra looks thoughtful; picking up a cashew, she says, "Hey, that Peter guy you ran into at the bar the other night, he's cute."

Theresa feels a slight lift in her mood at the mention of Peter. "Is he?" she doesn't like to comment on a client's looks.

"Oh, *okay*, you hadn't noticed because he's in the *client zone*." Nyra's hand goes up, dismissing her statement. "Well, for your information, he's *hot*. And he's fit. You can see that. I just wanted to touch his arm."

"You wanted to touch his arm?" Theresa laughs this off, experiencing a sensation of... is it jealousy? That's problematic. Does she have a crush on her client?

"He wore that golf tee like a *pro*. His arms are beautiful." Nyra has always loved men in T-shirts and jeans. That is apparently still her go-to. "You know what I like," she winks at Theresa.

"Well, you have a beautiful family that I think trump a pair of arms," Theresa finds herself discouraging her best friend but not because she believes Nyra's life would benefit from it, but rather because Theresa is experiencing some powerful jealousy over Nyra's interest in Peter. Maybe she's just being protective of them both.

"Right, but my husband's arms aren't attached to that lean, muscled body. I bet when Peter hugs that mousey little friend of his, she knows it." Now Nyra is being crude, Theresa thinks. "I could bury my face in his chest while his hug lingers."

"Okay, Nyra, fantasy's aside, he is my client, and I don't date my clients," Theresa wants this line of conversation to stop. She's feeling slightly warmer than a moment ago and removes her light sweater.

"Hey, you may not need the visual fantasies, but when I crawl into bed with Duke, it's the only way I can bring myself to let him touch me." Nyra lifts her glass with a sly smile and winks again.

"Oh, Nyra, I didn't know you were having problems like that," Theresa presses for more information, hoping to leave the Peter conversation in the past. "A lot of couples with children go through this. How long has this been going on?"

Nyra looks at Theresa with a sigh. "Like, three years?"

"What's put you off of Duke?"

"We're just not there anymore, you know?"

Theresa doesn't know and wishes she had a little more experience with long-term relationships so she could help her friend. Still, she has her training. "It's probably got to do with the kids. You're feeling trapped."

"It has a *lot* to do with the kids, Tree, but more to do with the fact that Duke and me, we don't talk anymore." Nyra helps herself to more of the wine.

"You guys are probably just burned out. You should leave the kids with Duke's parents and take a trip," Theresa knows this must sound easier than it is.

Nyra lets out another sigh. "We could, but I'm not sure a trip will fix what's broken. He doesn't look at me like that anymore, and frankly, I don't' know if I'm even in love anymore."

Theresa has only experienced the love of family and friends. She has never been *in love*. "Oh, Nyra, I'm sure that's not true. He's given you three beautiful children and a secure life. Are you wanting to go back to work?"

Nyra studies her glass, watching the wine swirl inside it, dismissing Theresa's question. "This *wine* has better legs than Duke." She looks up and allows herself a sarcastic smile. Theresa places a hand on her friend's shoulder.

"Surely there's more to love than arms and legs," she says with a sympathetic smile. "You guys were always the couple to be admired."

"We still are," Nyra pats Theresa's hand. "From all outside appearances, anyway. But everything else, it's just so, blah, you know?"

Again, Theresa doesn't know but wonders whether she and Peter might have a chance. She shakes off the forbidden thought and refocuses. "I can't believe everything on Facebook and Instagram is a show."

"They're not, but they certainly aren't a true representation of our lives."

"None are, I imagine," Theresa says, "but I think they speak to the good times. You guys have good times. Maybe you should focus on those and -"

"He's a great father," Nyra interrupts. "He offers stability and wisdom and all that." Nyra's attention returns to her glass. "You know, when we went out the other night, it felt like I was revisiting a time I'm not allowed to have anymore. Like the best years are gone. Freedom and self-reliance."

"We can go out whenever you want. Duke will watch the boys, and you'll have that again." Theresa tells her. "Trust me, being alone isn't all it's cracked up to be. Idle hands and all that ..."

"I know what I'd do with those idle hands," Nyra motions with a fist to her mouth and tongue in her cheek.

Theresa feels slightly embarrassed by the action and laughs it off. "Why don't you talk with Duke then?" Theresa is starting to realize Nyra doesn't want to talk about her husband. She wants someone to tell her to leave her husband. Theresa wouldn't be that friend. She had been a bridesmaid at their wedding. She'd witnessed each of their sons come into the world. She has enjoyed Nyra's friendship through all of it and felt protective of her happiness in that family setting. But maybe she is wrong to want that for her. Perhaps she's projecting or living vicariously.

"Sex is important in a relationship, Tree. I don't fault him for being bored, but I'd like to feel attractive again."

"To Duke?"

Nyra takes a moment to contemplate the question, painted fingertip rounding the edge of the glass. "Yes, to Duke, that would be nice. To other men. I feel like I jumped into my life and popped out a few babies, and now what?"

"Now you work at it. It came easy for you, but isn't that what love is? Easy?" Theresa feels another pang of excitement saying this. Peter excites her. Is that like love?

"Easy come, easy go," Nyra smiles again, but Theresa notices it's a sad smile this time. She's thinking about Duke. She takes another long sip.

"Consider a conversation before you decide to look outside the marriage, Nyra; promise me that. You guys are worth it."

Nyra smiles brightly now, but it could all be for show. Either way, perhaps she needed a friend to talk her out of the ideas poisoning her thoughts.

"You're a good friend, Tree." Nyra stands and finishes her glass. "I'd better relieve the in-laws." She picks up her bag from the stool and hugs her friend.

Theresa is left to consult her unexpected feelings as they arose about Peter. She can't be in love. That seems terribly quick. She empathizes with Peter; she doesn't *love* him. He's in a bad way and working through his past to build a better future. He's met a girl - Clare, who had introduced her to Peter. Stranger things have happened. His past lives, for instance. They have been brutal to relive but necessary, in her opinion. Necessary for Peter to improve his present. Peter, she thinks; his name alone prompts feelings she is ill-equipped to deal with.

No, she tells herself, I'm helping him. *I'm not looking for a relationship. I'm treating him. He's a client.* But this isn't making her feel any better about the unexpected sensation the memory of him produces.

Chapter 21

Peter joins Theresa in her treatment room, placing himself on the lounge. He's feeling nervous, but mostly he feels vulnerable. The robbery and the visit to the police station both play on his mind. He explains both events to Theresa, having experienced multiple panic attacks over the last few days. Each one seems triggered by the bookstore, a police siren, an officer walking his beat.

"You're innocent of the crime," Theresa says confidently, making Peter more comfortable.

He nods at this. "Of course, I'm not a monster. Even if I experienced the fugue, it's not in me to take a life like that." Peter replies. "Though I worry that my military background may make me a suspect."

"Let's not dwell on these events, Peter. Is it *possible* or *probable* that you'll be fingered for the crime?"

Peter takes a moment to consider the question. "Possible?"

"Sure, but very unlikely that it's probable. So don't waste your time worrying about it. Even probable, by definition, isn't proof."

"That's a curious way of thinking," Peter says, still trying to understand the difference.

"You don't want to speculate - is what I'm telling you. Divergent thinking will get you nowhere. Convergent thinking – using logic, will help deflect any concerns you have over the outcome."

"I'll remember that." Peter feels lighter from the conversation and pulls the weighted blanket up his torso.

"Good, I'll offer a cleanse of your energies, and we'll get started." Theresa lowers the lighting, and Peter experiences a chill. He rests his head against the plush lounge. Chimes are introduced next as Theresa lays hands above Peter's throat to even out his energy. "I'm going to lead with reiki focusing on the throat chakra, and then we'll begin the regression," she whispers.

His body senses Theresa's energy and submits to her. The sensations Peter experiences are of being lightly touched by thousands of fingertips as they brush over every nerve ending, knowing Theresa isn't touching him at all.

Peter finds himself again with a choice. Not so much a choice as a calling. The call of gravity pulls him toward a door meant to serve him in his present by revealing a past he can learn from.

The imaginary hallway stretches out before him like an elastic band pulled too tight. It begins to shudder, and a door to his immediate left vibrates to match his frequency. This is when the pull of gravity ensnares his ethereal form, drawing him closer to the door until it opens, and he is driven into a past his conscious mind no longer identifies with.

The timeline seems fuzzy. Peter looks at his feet as instructed and comments on the footwear. It's all at once foreign and familiar to him. "Lady's shoes," he mumbles. This is a switch. He's a woman? "I'm a woman."

He describes the setting and moves to a mirror. His reflection is appealing in a 19th-century kind of way. He explains that he is in Russia and is to be paraded in front of single men who come from wealthy backgrounds on this very evening. Young, old, rich, it is not what he wants. Peter begins to think in the feminine and refers to himself as such. Her name is Kristina, and she lives on a fine estate on land owned by her family for generations. She is one of many women of age being presented tonight at a ball in her father's home. Peter looks out his second-floor window to observe diplomats and royalty emerge from their carriages in an orderly fashion, their footmen opening doors and calling out names.

Peter is discouraged. Why? Because Kristina has other ideas. She will flee the spectacle at the end of the evening and meet her lover, who will be waiting for her at the great oak on the east end of her family's property.

She and Feliks have been meeting for months like this. He is the woodsman on the property, employed by her family. Peter feels his heart pound faster thinking of the young Feliks, his lean muscled form and thick, powerful hands pressing against her. She was no longer a virgin, which would prove problematic for the aristocracy looking her over as potential marriage material.

Peter feels a tear tracing down his cheek. Kristina could not forsake Feliks or herself the opportunity for a lifetime of happiness. Her parents would stop her if they knew her intentions. Still, she must make a show of it tonight to draw any suspicions away from her plan.

Peter feels the depth of Kristina's love for Feliks. The sensation fills his chest. He has never been in love himself. Kristina looks about her room and eyes the bag she will take with her to the oak tree. It is hidden even from her maid. No one can know.

Once summoned, Kristina manages a final review in her mirror. She stands tall and runs her palms over her torso, fitted tightly into her corset. Her palms are wet with nerves. Her hair and make-up look perfect. She will draw much attention from the nobility and must remember her manners. It will be over soon enough, Peter thinks. Then she will be happy.

The roar of voices below makes her hesitate at the top of the staircase. She's no stranger to these large gatherings, music, food, and dancing, but tonight is different. Tonight will be her last. She will not miss them; she convinces herself, not once she is laying in Feliks's arms many miles removed from her palatial home. He will provide for her, and she for him. They will make babies, and she will be a mother and Feliks a father. She is in love, and Feliks loves her. There is no going back. Nothing will stand between them.

"My daughter, Kristina," her father announces as she steps off the winding staircase to greet the assembled guests. She admits two of the younger men are quite fetching, but her heart is spoken for. An older man, as old as her father, takes her hand and kisses the lace of her glove. She curtseys and smiles, but not too brightly. She would not wish to share this man's bed. The others follow suit and move on to the next girl being presented.

Kristina takes a full glass from the tray of a passing servant and drinks thirstily. A fire warms the guests, and Kristina avails herself to one dance after another, getting to know her suitors as they take their turns.

Her mother, Peter explains, is radiant next to her father. This is the moment her parents have dreamed of, and she would be crushing that dream in mere hours. It does not make her feel good, but neither does the prospect of sharing her life with someone she does not love. Kristina looks up at the chandelier but only sees Feliks's face there in its brilliance and drops her gaze, smiling. Mistakenly, a young man assumes the smile for him and slides up beside Kristina, with a glass of champagne for her.

She nods and graciously accepts the glass. The boy becomes assertive with her, leading Kristina to a couch by the elbow. They sit, and he explains his intentions. He rhymes off his many titles and wants, but Peter finds himself still in the glow of Feliks's face. Kristina is unwavering in her love and cannot wait to escape this nonsense and get back to him.

The party ends eventually, to Kristina's great relief. She returns to her room after hugging her parents tightly. She will miss them greatly but is eighteen and in love and will not be talked out of it as if she were experiencing some silly flight of fancy. That's what her father would tell her, and her mother would agree.

Peter finds himself slipping out of the dress with the help of his maid and into a nightgown. She thanks the girl and sends her away. Next, she changes into something more suitable to flee, bagging her nightgown. She pours her jewelry into the bag and a large sum of rubles. They will not want for much before Feliks secures a new job. Shoes and tiaras are next. She places her delicate feet into appropriate boots for the journey and throws a heavy jacket over her shoulders. Everything has been planned. Everything is going perfectly to that plan. Kristina dares a look out her window and watches the last of the carriages depart.

She's trusted no one with this escape. Her maid doesn't even know about Feliks, and she tells her everything. The house will soon be dark to match the night, and Kristina will abscond from this privileged life. Is she being naïve? Perhaps, she knows little of the world, but Feliks is from that world, not this one. He will make her safe. He will make her happy.

As the servants depart for their quarters and her parents sleep soundly in a haze of champagne, Kristina creeps through the ancient hallways and staircase to slip out the cook's door. Peter admits his heart is racing as Kristina rushes through the open grass fields between the majestic trees that dot the landscape. There is not even a moon in the sky to give her up. The bag is heavy, but she makes excellent time crossing the expansive yard. The oak is in sight, and she tumbles into Feliks's waiting arms.

Feliks kisses her deeply, and Kristina returns the passionate embrace, holding onto Feliks like he is her lifeboat. They stay like this for some time.

"I'm sorry," Feliks tells her as they break their embrace. "I'm so sorry."

Peter is mystified over Feliks's apology. "What have you to apologize for?" Peter feels breathless. Anxiety rears up in Kristina like a fire in her belly. It becomes smoke in her chest, and she gasps. Tears flow freely as Feliks is pulled away by two of her father's footmen. They move to their left to reveal her father.

"You're a silly girl, Kristina," he is utterly disappointed in her. "There can be no more of this."

Peter is caught up in the moment, and Kristina is speechless.

"You think us clueless to your affair, but we have never been so. Your mother suggested we stop it much earlier than tonight, but I wanted to give you that opportunity. It seems I was wrong in my attitudes toward you."

"Oh, father, please, let me go; I love Feliks. I can't do what you ask," Peter is shaking from the possibility he will never be allowed to live out her dream.

Peter explains that Kristina's father now looks to Feliks and nods. Feliks steps forward and cruelly tells Kristina that he does not love her and is only using her.

Kristina cries out at this. *That's not true. I know what we have. I know it's not true.* But whether it was or wasn't, Feliks leaves the scene as Kristina's father returns her to her room in the stately house, resembling more a prison than a home now.

Theresa brings Peter out of the regression and sighs as she leans back into her seat.

"You mentioned Feliks's face more than once. Did you capture who he is in this life?"

Peter is groggy and upset over the love lost between Kristina and Feliks. "Do you think they ever found one another again?"

"Whether they did or didn't isn't why you experienced this traumatic scene. What you were meant to encounter, you did. It's a slice of life. Not an end." She speaks calmly to ease Peter's return to the present.

"I don't believe what he'd said," Peter sits up, the weighted blanket falling to the floor. "They'd frightened him into saying that."

"Maybe, but before you lose the moment, did you recognize anyone in Feliks's eyes?"

Peter sits in contemplation. Did he? He was so engaged with the life he hadn't bothered to consider who Feliks might be in the present.

"I don't think so," he finally admits. "Maybe. I'll have to think about it." *Could it be Clare?* He doesn't want to tell Theresa this. It would be embarrassing, and she would caution him against seeing her again. He is enjoying their time together and doesn't want it to end. He's not in love or anything. Not if love feels like what Kristina felt for Feliks. That was powerful. He's sad over their loss.

"You may discover this life will play out in the days to come," Theresa tells him. "We witnessed your lover betray your feelings. Your parent's love is another aspect to deliberate on. I mean, *Kristina's* parents. Perhaps you saw someone in the present in their eyes?"

Peter shakes his head slowly. "I don't think it was about her relationship with her parents. It doesn't feel like that to me."

"Then let it percolate. Listen to the recording I've just texted you. Review your feelings, and we'll discuss it again." She stands, and Peter follows her lead. "If something rises to the surface, you can text me. We can address it sooner if you need to."

"Thank you," Peter lets himself out the front door and thoughtfully strolls down the residential street, boards the bus, and goes home.

Chapter 22

Detective Harlow wakes to his mobile phone ringing. It's a distinctive ring reserved for one person: his ex-wife. The call sends him reeling out of a dream, his large hand slamming down upon the phone, thick fingers grasping it and pulling it to his ear. He responded as he'd always done, quickly when his wife called - allowing no more than two rings before he answered.

"Tiff?" His voice cracks under the weight of speaking her name aloud. "What's wrong?" He can think of no other reason she'd call. He sits up in bed, scratching at his chest.

"It's Oscar," she tells him, Harlow catching the distress in her voice. Oscar is their shared Dachshund. He's just three years old. Harlow hasn't seen Oscar in months. Not his choice, but he let Tiff keep him longer and longer until he stopped asking to see him. Still, he loves the little noodle.

"Something's wrong with Oscar?" *Does she want money? Is he sick?*

"He's run off," she tells him. He remembers the way she could be with the dog; overprotective, coddling, dressing him up in ridiculous outfits for every occasion. Harlow let her have her fun with Oscar, but when they were alone, he commiserated with the dog while they watched the 11 o'clock news, and Tiff was fast asleep.

"When?" Harlow remembers the loving pet who crashed on his lap almost every night when they were together. *Why can't she call with good news?*

"In the night, I - I had a friend over, and I think they left the screen door open when they left."

A *friend*, one who left in the middle of the night, no doubt. *Why can't she get her life together? Why did she leave him for that?* "I've got the day off," he tells her, "I could help you look for him."

"Would you?" She sounds relieved. "I'm sure he hasn't wandered far, but you remember how curious he can be."

Harlow had forgotten Oscar's curious nature, not having seen him in over five months. The idea that he might be in trouble or stolen has the detective out of bed and rooting through the 'to-be-washed' pile in the corner of his room for a pair of jeans. "I'll meet you at your place in twenty," he says, dropping the phone on his bed and pulling on his pants.

This is a trigger, he thinks, switching on the coffee maker as he moves through the kitchen to the bathroom. *She hasn't let me see Oscar in months, but she comes calling when he's in trouble.* It's the first time he's heard from her in over three months. It's funny how a fur baby can keep you connected when nothing else does. He almost regrets having bought Oscar for that very reason. He accepted that she reneged on his visitation rights with Oscar after the split. It steeled him against her.

Now, this. He pours his coffee and rushes out the door, speeding off in his Dodge Charger to search for his dog. Memories of the noodle (his nickname for Oscar) run through his mind as he navigates the Sunday morning traffic. They'd gotten him when he was just 12 weeks old. He was impossibly cute. They named him Oscar because he is a wiener dog. Too obvious? Yeah. He grew up long and thin, resembling a noodle more than a wiener to Harlow.

At Tiff's place, he finds her bent over in the shrubs in front of her small, Tudor-style home. She's calling his name and frantically pushing through the dense foliage.

"Tiff, I'm here. Where haven't you looked?" Harlow drains his coffee, feeling human again, stopping a few feet from his ex-wife. *She looks ragged. I probably shouldn't mention that.*

"I've just kept to the property," she looks him in the eye, "thank you for coming." Harlow nods.

"I'll start moving down the street. If you find him, call me. I'll do the same." Shit, if something's happened to Oscar, Harlow thinks he'll take it badly. No, he knows he will. The noodle's face is top of mind as he calls Oscar's name and knocks on doors.

The morning gives way to the afternoon, and the desperate parents meet up at Tiff's once more. Neither has had any luck. Harlow knows Dachshunds are a breed that is often stolen and resold for thousands. He hates the idea Oscar might never see home again.

Regardless of whether he has the chance to hold his dog again, he'd like for Oscar to be with his mom.

"Oscar!" Tiff's relieved voice shouts as Harlow walks dejectedly up the drive. He turns to where her attention is focused, and there is Oscar, running on his tiny legs to catch up. He bends down and catches the noodle as he springs into Harlow's arms, tail going a mile a minute. Harlow's heart slams against his chest as if jolted back to life.

"Hey, Noodle!" He says excitedly, accepting wet kisses from his boy. "You scared us, buddy," Harlow turns to see Tiff with her hands covering her mouth and tears welling up. Harlow smiles cheerfully, a smile only Oscar can coax out of him. Usually, he can only manage a sardonic smirk, but everything is genuine with Oscar. His face feels the burn of the authentic grin, but it's comforting, and he allows it.

Tiff approaches tentatively and puts her arms out to receive Oscar. Harlow hands him over. She hugs him too tightly. They have words in whispers, and she turns to take him inside. "Did you want to visit for a bit?"

"Sure," Harlow doesn't feel like he's had enough time with Oscar yet. Inside, the house is well kept, and he sits on what was their shared couch. Still comfortable.

"Can I get you anything? A drink?" Harlow notices the time - it's well after 12, and he nods as Oscar is placed next to him on the couch. This was the same couch they'd watch the 11 o'clock news on together. Oscar climbs onto his lap, circles twice, and then collapses heavily there. Harlow rubs the back of his head, flips a floppy ear over, and whispers how scared they were.

Tiff returns with a beer for each of them. "That was all you," she tells him, sitting in a chair across the coffee table. "I think he responded to your voice. Like he remembers you."

"Yeah," Harlow sips his beer and grunts, staring down at the sleeping Oscar. "Lots of dark scenarios going through my head," he submits.

"Are there any other kind in that head of yours?" She says it with humor, but Harlow knows she means it. It's what drove them apart, she'd told him.

"Ah, well, yes, but I hate when I'm right. Thankfully, not this time." He tips his head to drink.

"So, how are you? I'm sorry this is how I invite you over, but -"

"Never mind that you did the right thing calling me. I'm good. My place could use a woman's touch, but otherwise good."

"How's work?"

Harlow nods, looking up at her. "You stopped asking that years ago."

"I was too involved then. Now, we're just friends, talking."

Why do women always want to be friends after? "Sure, work is fine. Same shit. You don't want to hear about it." He finishes his beer and lifts Oscar gently from his lap, placing him on the couch.

"Maybe you'd like to take Oscar with you? Have him for the week? I know we haven't done that in a while." She says, standing, looking sheepish.

Harlow considers it, but with his caseload, he feels he won't be able to give Oscar the attention he deserves. "Can I have a raincheck on that?"

"Sure," Tiff nods, crossing her arms. "Thanks again, and let me know when you'd like to take him. I've been selfish."

Harlow nods again; his mouth opens but no words form, and he exits the house. He thinks about his time with Tiffany on the car ride home, in the shower, and as he tries to focus on a television show. He eyes the lighter on the coffee table and picks it up.

The satisfying snap ignites the flame, and he watches it consume the oxygen around him. He takes an unsteady breath and studies the light show dancing across his hand. It's his ex-wife. She – the flame – approaches his outstretched arm and licks a fiery tongue at his exposed flesh. It burns steadily, Harlow letting it linger a little longer than usual.

Chapter 23

Clare has been uncharacteristically absent since the traumatic robbery. Her texts have been short and lacking any charm. Peter feels withdrawn - depressive thoughts trickle into his day-to-day. Sleep is hard to come by, and he's noticed he's become far too vigilant over checking and rechecking his locks.

His robber is dead; Peter uses this information to put his mind at ease. He repeats this fact to himself. Still, he worries. That's the PTSD again. He was never a worrier before Afghanistan. He recognizes the warning signs, and this helps him regain focus. The bookstore has been quiet too. Sanderson hasn't been back. He must be traveling again, or maybe he's made up with his wife? Whatever the reason, it's comforting not to have to deal with him while he's trying to recover from the event.

His cell phone rings, and he fishes it out of his jeans pocket. It's Clare. His heart falls to his stomach. This is a good sign, though; she hasn't initiated a chat since. He reads the text:

I just wanted to apologize. I'm not mad at you. I know it must seem that way. I'm still a little frazzled. I've been off work a few days now and starting to feel like myself again. I entered counseling and am making headway. I don't want to lose you. I've enjoyed our time together.

Okay, Peter thinks, his heart racing, that's not all bad. He feels responsible for her needing to seek counseling but is glad she's doing it. He texts her the same. He also asks when she might like to get together again, hope creeping in like a stranger.

It takes a few moments for Clare to respond, but she does. He wipes his sweating palms on his jeans and retrieves his phone.

I'm being asked to stay clear of the shop, she responds. His heart further embeds itself in his guts. But maybe we meet up at 'Quoth the Raven' again?

Peter replies with a yes; when? Is that too needy? He hopes not. He doesn't want to play games with her, though. He wants her to know she's important to him.

Tomorrow night? She texts back. He confirms a time and slumps into one of the high-backed chairs in front of the fireplace in the bookstore. He sighs heavily, wishing they didn't have this barrier between them. He is hoping that tomorrow night they will be able to pick up where they left off. *Was that possible?* He worries it won't be like it was. *Will this shared trauma pull them apart or bring them together on a deeper level?* That is yet to be seen.

Peter recalls his therapy and something the Sergeant had said in Group when another Vet who has PTSD mentioned how she just wanted to feel normal again. *What's normal?* The Sergeant asked. *Everyone is fucked up to varying degrees. It's how we react that makes the difference.* Triggers are reminders of the trauma, and how we deal with them is how we move past them. It's called cognitive behavioral therapy. Peter has acquired many tools to manage his PTSD through this treatment, but it's an ongoing battle to change the way you think and remember events. Still, it has given him skills to manage his life thus far.

It's been a week, and he's due to see Theresa again tonight. Nothing had surfaced from the last regression when he was Kristina from Russia. He has no waking memories of dreams. This is where Theresa thought he might find answers, where he could identify the eyes of Kristina's lover, Feliks. He'd reneged on his feelings for her at a moment when she had been sure of his intentions. It was a jarring and devastating blow. Would he suffer a similar event tomorrow night with Clare?

Clare... her elfin smile and bright eyes stare back at him in his memory. He experiences an uncanny sense of foreboding there. "It's you," he says aloud, knowing with certainty Feliks was Clare in another life. This new knowledge forces him deeper into the leather, high-backed chair, sinking into its soft grip. *Could it be?* All hope is dashed at their reconnecting. He feels defeated, his palms burning. He is guilty of letting this happen. He continues to wring his hands until his fingers crack under the pressure he's applying.

He makes a conscious effort to alter his waning beliefs. *Is it possible or probable?* Theresa's words offer a comforting reprieve. It's certainly *possible*, but would she have reached out to meet if she planned to end things? No, he postulates.

He's been killing time before his walk to the bus stop. It's now 6:30, and he stands, shaking out the anxiety building in his chest and arms. He pockets his phone and pulls out his keys.

Theresa welcomes Peter back with her damaged smile, ushering him into the treatment room. He takes his place on the lounge and gathers up the weighted blanket.

"Have you discovered anything more about your last regression?" She sits with the clipboard resting on her lap.

Peter suffers indecision. He's apprehensive over telling her about the relationship Clare shares with Feliks. It frightens him. As Theresa supposed, if people come back to repeat offenses, he would be cautioned against seeing her tomorrow night. That would not do. But withholding information from his therapist doesn't seem helpful either. Peter simply nods.

"That's good, Peter," Theresa encourages more from him. "What connections have you made?"

"He's Clare," Peter confesses gravely, hands firmly clasped together under the weight of the blanket. He studies its patterns, afraid to meet Theresa's gaze.

"This is upsetting you."

Peter nods, his head not lifting. "I was torn over telling you."

"I understand, of course; she's been a great comfort of late."

"You'll want me to distance myself from her," Peter says joylessly.

"Oh, Peter, I'm not going to advise you against seeing her again," Theresa replies earnestly. "Perhaps she will show you compassion in this life."

Peter senses a false tone to her response. She doesn't believe that. "You sound unsure."

"You asked me once if a person couldn't come back in a different role, a helpful role," Theresa reminds him. "Have you experienced that yet?"

Peter shakes his head, no. "So, you don't believe any good will come of my being with Clare."

"Not at all; I'm only asking you to look at the patterns we've already experienced. Your Mr. Sanderson has been a source of stress; your book club patron was a thief -"

"Right, and my girlfriend is a soul-crushing monster," Peter finishes the model for her. "But I don't want to see her that way."

"And I'm not asking you to," Theresa becomes animated. "There is good in Clare. She's been nothing but good to you. Has the robbery become a problem for the two of you?"

"Yes, it's changed things. She's gone to counseling because of it. She's been distant."

"That's a very normal response to a trauma, Peter."

"She did reach out today, though. We made plans to meet tomorrow night." Peter lifts his head to assess Theresa's reaction.

"Good," she leans forward in her chair and nods. "Then she wants to return to that connection."

"Do you think?" Peter feels suddenly optimistic.

"I think she's worth the effort, Peter." She leans back again and marks something down on her clipboard.

"Okay, good," this was an unexpected reaction from his therapist.

"I'm on your side, remember. I want you to explore your possibilities. If you find even a modicum of joy while you're together – however long that may be, it is to your benefit, not detriment."

Peter understands. If he and Clare were to continue a relationship for a few months more or a few years, it would be far better than stopping it now to avoid the possibility of a painful end in the future.

"Live in the now but appreciate what the past has to show you," Theresa explains. "And how have *you* coped with the robbery? Are you managing?"

"I think so. I use what I've learned," Peter replies confidently. "The worst of it has been the disconnect I've felt the past few days with Clare."

"Then approach tomorrow night with an open heart and understanding toward her sensitivities over the event. She may seem withdrawn, but she's trying."

Peter agrees. "I can do that." He settles into the lounge, the stress of the conversation dissolving. He feels safe under Theresa's spell as she moves her hands above him, aligning his energies. He closes his eyes and listens to her instructions.

In a short time, Peter is back in the hall of doorways, floating through the narrow space. Doors seem to shimmer beside him as he moves through the unending hall. He experiences no anxiety here. He is at the mercy of his unconscious, evaluating the many lives he has experienced to locate the one that will heal him or offer direction in this life.

His focus turns to an unassuming door that could be attached to a house in the present. This past will not be too far removed from his present. He is pulled beyond the screen door and immediately finds himself pushing back through it.

"I'm angry," Peter relays, "he's done it again. He's cheated!"

"Who's cheated, Peter?"

"Sydney," he says through clenched teeth. "I can't trust a thing he says. *Why* do I keep going back?"

"Peter, this has happened in the past," Theresa reminds him. "Remember, this is not happening to you now. It can't hurt you. It can only serve to help you."

Peter listens, and the anger subsides. "I'm gone for two days on a business trip, and he can't wait to bed another man."

"Look at your feet, Peter."

He explains the footwear. Red, Adidas Gazelles. Pristine condition, he adds. "My boyfriend is an asshole."

He delves into their rocky relationship. Love is fickle. Love is unkind. Peter's name is Raymond, and he and Sydney had been together two years after meeting at a bathhouse in Toronto. They'd been involved in the police raids in 1981, which drove the Gay Pride movement later that year. In their first year together, the two were inseparable, becoming heavily involved in the movement.

A trip to San Francisco led Raymond to open a bookstore in Toronto in 1982, where the couple entered a business relationship to complement their romantic one. Raymond managed the book fairs and marketing while Sydney managed the day-to-day at the shop.

Being away as often as he was had become a problem as Sydney felt slighted. Their heated arguments ended in make-up sex, but the writing was on the wall. The relationship was becoming unstable. Sydney felt empowered sleeping around while Raymond kept the business afloat. Now, this. The second time he'd walked in on his boyfriend with another man.

"It's unconscionable," Peter explains. "We can't have it both ways. We can't do this anymore."

"And so, you left him?"

"Yes," Peter's voice is a whisper. "I couldn't trust him anymore."

"And how did that work out?"

"Sydney died a year later. Complications from AIDS."

"Oh, I'm so sorry, Peter," Theresa senses Peter's dismay. "You still loved him."

"Yes, I hadn't moved on. I bought him out of the bookstore and never saw him again. I heard through the grapevine he'd contracted AIDS and had myself checked out. It wasn't an easy time. A few months later, I heard he'd died."

"Do you regret not seeing him again?"

"I regret many things where Syd was involved, but that was the worst."

"You were dealing with feelings of betrayal," she tells him. "You can't blame yourself for not reconnecting."

"No, but I never recovered from the loss."

Theresa asks the burning question with as much tact as she can muster, "when you look at Sydney, do you recognize him?"

Peter releases a single tear. "It's Clare."

167

Theresa is silent for a long moment as they both process this information. "Peter, I'd like you to come back to the present. In one... two... three."

Peter wipes his cheek, where the tear is still fresh. "That's 2 and 0 for Clare, I guess."

"I won't tell you how to proceed with your relationship, Peter," Theresa says. "These things are often more complicated -"

"I will see her tomorrow night," Peter interrupts, sniffing and clearing his throat. "I'll see her."

Theresa nods, and Peter appreciates the melancholy in her gaze. But there's something else, a strength she's passing on to him. They finish the session in quiet contemplation. Theresa leads him out the front door, and Peter moves through the darkened street, head down, considering how he'll approach Clare the following day.

Chapter 24

A missing person's call isn't something Harlow gets a lot of. He's only assisted in missing person's cases when his load was light. Today, this isn't the case with a serial murderer on a rampage, but this missing person's case shares a commonality with his own.

Detective Harlow arrives at the scene where forensics is already sweeping the area. He slips on a pair of polypropylene shoe covers and latex-free gloves. The apartment is in a state of mild disarray; a broken vase here, an overturned plant there - blood on the couch that might amount to brief a nosebleed.

"Detective Sysco," Harlow greets the lead investigator for missing persons as she snaps photos of the scene with her iPhone.

She's an attractive woman Harlow has longed to work with again in this capacity. They would be working closely on this missing person because of the shared link to his case. He watches her turn to meet his gaze, her blonde hair pulled tight into a high ponytail, moving over her left shoulder as if in slow motion. Her turquoise eyes burn into his for a moment before long lashes blink away their enchanting spell, snapping him out of his reverie.

"Detective," she replies, voice carrying over the melee of activity in the apartment. "It's good to see you again, though I'm sorry it's always under these circumstances." She hands him the bagged note.

Harlow nods, briefly wondering whether she might like to meet outside of work someday. His forefinger touches Sysco's as he receives the baggie. They experience a static shock between them. Sysco smiles, pulling her hand back suddenly. Harlow notices how her lips part somewhat, and the tight skin between her eyebrows furrows ever so slightly.

As Harlow reviews the note, he recalls the others. They seem identical, but that would have to be confirmed by forensics. The same cryptic message. Maybe this time, the killer screwed up, he thinks.

"I appreciate the call, Detective," Harlow hands the note off to one of the forensics. "Let me know the minute you know," he tells the officer, who nods and rushes away with the evidence. Harlow turns back to Sysco.

"This doesn't exactly align with your serial killer's MO," she states, narrowing her eyes at her phone's screen and snapping another picture.

"Two outta three, some would take those odds," Harlow jokes. Sysco looks up at him, unimpressed. Harlow clears his throat. "But you're right; this is out of character for our killer. This could be the break we've been hoping for."

"I hope for her sake it is." Sysco squats down to identify a dust bunny.

"That the victim is a woman this time is also uncharacteristic. So far, it's been men." Harlow moves past the attractive detective toward a photograph on a buffet. He picks it up, studying the face set upon a field of sunflowers. "This is her? This is our victim?"

Sysco looks up and nods. "Pretty, isn't she?"

In a mousey kind of way, Harlow considers and then recognizes the woman. He snaps up his phone and reviews his messages. "Clare Hastings," he announces.

"That's right, we sent you her information," Detective Sysco stands.

"She was brought into the station, concerning the last victim, with her boyfriend -" Harlow stops himself.

"Boyfriend, eh?" Sysco watches Harlow, but he's looking right through her now.

"Call in for backup to secure the Bookaneer in Cornerstone Village on East Warren Avenue between Outer Dr. East and Cadieux," Harlow pushes past her. He apologizes. "This guy's admitted to being in the locality of the last murder, and that was confirmed on video surveillance. We haven't enough to bring him in, but this changes things."

Sysco lifts her phone to her ear and makes the call.

Harlow liked this Peter for the murders. His military background, his PTSD – or so he claimed – his quiet life nestled within the innocent façade of a bookstore. *This is his guy.* He speeds to meet the police presence at the shop, anxious to question Peter further on the whereabouts of Clare Hastings.

At the Bookaneer, Peter is startled to receive several police officers into his small shop. They begin shouting at him, guns drawn, ordering him to lay down on his belly, hands behind his head. He obeys, heart-pounding, anxiety peaking.

He is handcuffed and hauled to his feet as two terrified patrons are escorted out of the bookstore. They look back at him in dismay. He shakes his head, "t-this is a mistake."

"Is it?" It's that Detective Harlow who questioned him about the other night. Oh, God, had he done something? He didn't think so... Harlow directs the officers to place him in one of the high-backed chairs and seats himself in the other.

"I'm sorry we had to take such a strong position here, Mr. Banks, but we've discovered something very upsetting." He motions for the officer situated behind Peter to remove his cuffs.

Peter rubs at his hands and rolls his shoulders. He has never been detained before. It's more unpleasant than he'd imagined. *What have they discovered?* Anxiety over the whole episode has him feeling dizzy; his hands experience the encroaching pins and needles. Concentrate on your breathing, Peter, he tells himself.

"Your friend Clare," Harlow surprises Peter with the mention of Clare. "Where is she?"

"What? Why?"

"Because she's currently missing," the detective says bluntly. This forces Peter to straighten up in his chair.

"Missing? Who says she's missing?"

"Her mother, in fact. She's tried to reach her daughter for the past 30 hours, and when she couldn't, she called us. We sent a uniformed officer to her penthouse, and he found the door ajar and, well, you know what he found." Harlow's eyes burn into Peters.

"I know – what do you mean, *I know?*" Peter is beyond confused and now horrified over what they'd found.

"How about you just tell me where she is?"

"I – I don't know where she is." That's the truth. Clare had skipped out on their date the night before, and he hasn't been able to get a hold of her since. He explains this to the detective. "We'd made a date to meet up at 'Quoth the Raven,' that new spot downtown. She never showed. That was, uh, seven last night. I waited, I texted; you can ask anyone that was there. I sat at a table for over two hours."

"So, you were at this restaurant from 7 until 9? That can be corroborated?" Harlow asks, and Peter nods. "Where were you the rest of the day?"

"Here," Peter says, his mind wandering to dark scenarios. "I closed up at six and got on the bus about

6:15. Arrived at about 6:50. I came straight home on the bus. I guess about 9:45, I made it home."

Harlow's eyes narrow at Peter, and he leans back, taking a long breath Peter can hear. It's unsettling. "And you stayed here last night once you returned? No late-night strolls?"

Peter nods. "She never returned any of my texts. I even called her twice."

"Did that not alarm you?"

"We've been a bit off since the robbery," Peter hates to admit it, but he feels Clare had brushed him off.

"So, your relationship is on the rocks," the statement seems leading.

"It hadn't been what it was before the armed robbery," Peter admits. "We were going to meet last night to discuss it."

"This was Clare's idea?"

"That's right," Peter is becoming worried for Clare's safety. "Are you going to find her?"

"Do you know where she is?" Harlow asks again. Peter just shakes his head. "We're going to keep you at the station if that's alright with you."

"A–am I under arrest?"

Harlow looks around the shop and turns to Peter, "No, but I'd rather keep you close than have you become a victim yourself."

"*Victim?* Is that what you think Clare is? A victim?"

"She's missing, and we have reason to believe she's in danger. You could also be in danger," Harlow is changing tactics on Peter, he notices. He wants to keep him close, not safe. But whatever he can do to help.

"I'll close up and get my things," Peter announces, and Harlow nods to the officer to follow.

Chapter 25

Clare never saw her attacker. She'd been sitting on her couch, mid-day, reviewing analytics she'd received from the marketing department at work. Her head wasn't in it, though. Her thoughts were with Peter. She'd been upset with herself over how she'd acted toward him the past few days. It wasn't Peter's fault she'd been caught up in an armed robbery. In fact, he'd been incredibly calm throughout the whole ordeal. Clare shudders to think how it might have gone without him there.

Caught up in the memory, Clare lit a candle to settle her nerves. The counseling she'd received had helped, and she was glad she reached out to Peter to suggest a meet-up. A smile crept across her face over the thought of seeing him again. She considered the time and stood to retrieve her phone from the kitchen counter.

A searing pain struck Clare in the back of the head, and her vision blurred as she stumbled and landed face down on her couch. She'd feared she'd had an aneurism.

Now awake and suffering the residual headache from the blow, Clare finds herself in a small room, possibly a basement, if the damp smell is any indication. She is tied to a chair, arms squeezed against her sides, hands behind her. Her calves are similarly tied and secured to the chair's legs.

"Hello," she manages a hoarse whisper and clears her throat. "Hello?" Clare feels utterly helpless. How could she have ended up here? Who would have done this to her? She runs through a series of possibilities but arrives at no one who would want to scare her like this. They'd *assaulted* her. They've hidden her away. This is a nightmare, she thinks as panic rises to meet the intensity of the pounding in her head.

It's so dark; she waits for her eyes to adjust. Slivers of muted light break up the darkness where blackout curtains must be drawn over the high-set windows. Her other senses work diligently to discern her location. She listens to the creaks and groans of the building above her. It's a basement, she surmises. Something scuttles across her foot, and she lets out a squeak of terror. Her mind fills with scenarios of being left to the rats. She hates rats. It's why she bought the penthouse suite. No rats. No possibility of rats. Now she shares a dark, dank basement with the greasy little monsters.

What have I done to deserve this? There's nothing I could have done to end up like this. She struggles again against the rough ropes expertly securing her to the chair. She tries to stand to see if the ropes will give a little but is afraid to fall over and have her face at the same level as the vermin.

Tears tumble quickly down her reddening face. Clare cries out to frighten the rats but also out of frustration. The chair bounces on its feet as she can't help but continue the struggle. I won't die like this, she tells herself. I won't. The chair feels made of metal, so she can't hope to break its back and wiggle free. Sweat stings her eyes as it moves past her thin eyebrows. She wants to scream again but considers her position.

I'm alone right now, save the rats; perhaps my captor should think me unconscious. What will they do to me when they learn I'm awake? They've been waiting for me to regain consciousness. Why? Why do this to me? I'm nobody. She is a young executive at a budding social media platform. *There could be no ransom for my life. My parents work two jobs each and live in a rental on the city's outskirts. There is no money.*

Clare becomes angry at the absurdity of it. This can't be for money, but if not money, what? Will she be sold to some uber-wealthy ex-pat on an island somewhere? Will she never see her family again? Peter? It's odd Peter comes to mind, she thinks. Peter, who she's only just met but has become increasingly fond of. Someone she could see herself with in the long term. *Would he be her knight in shining armor? Could he? He would be worried she hadn't shown up on their date. Was that last night? How long has it been?*

She wants answers but not from the person who's abducted her. She doesn't want to face them. *Who could they be? Why are they doing this?* She tries to rub the rope against the chair's back spindle where her wrists meet. It's painful, but it's something. She can't just sit here and do nothing.

Her breath catches in her throat as footfalls rain dust down on her from above. She coughs against her better judgment. Light pours into the basement down rickety-looking wooden steps from a door above.

A singular figure takes one methodical step at a time as they descend the staircase. Once they reach the cracked cement floor, Clare's frantic gaze settles on an ambiguous character dressed in baggy, dark clothing, a balaclava over their face. Her heart sinks, and she holds her breath.

Chapter 26

Detective Harlow broods over the evidence on his desk. The hotel surveillance he'd sent to the forensics team offers a brief interaction with the first victim and a person dressed in a dark, lumpy outfit. They are wearing a heavy, black hat as they stop to proposition the victim just off center of the frame at the front entrance to the hotel. The victim seems interested. He's identifiable from the work forensics has done to improve the digital imaging and his hair, large stature, and the clothes he'd died in. The suspect, unfortunately, is unrecognizable. Though it's exciting for Harlow to have a suspect, he curses the foresight they'd had in camouflaging themselves.

The bartender, Charlotte, had also identified the victim in the video, so he's got that going for him. He watches for the tenth time as the suspect leads the victim out of the frame by the arm. Is it a woman? As Charlotte had mentioned, Harlow believes a man on the prowl might easily be lured away by a woman. He was likely drunk, though, as the night manager's email suggested by the drinks purchased so that the woman could have been a man. Hell, maybe the victim didn't have a preference. Forensics noted the suspect's gait, and the FBI agent also commented on this. It looks exaggerated, practiced, so not to give them away in their day-to-day, but the team would look for additional footage denoting the gait in the video before this one to see if they could capture an image of the suspect without their costume on. They'd both admitted it was a long shot.

It's clear from the home security footage that the victim drove home. So, where is the suspect? *Had they hidden in the backseat? Then what? The suspect jabbed the needle into the victim, incapacitating him, staged the murder, and left their calling card? Sure, but what's the motive? The motive is the real mystery.* If he could unravel that, he might have a better chance of identifying the suspect. They have the height and projected weight of the suspect from the video but little else. It's like the perp knew where to stand to avoid recognition.

He reviews the video again from the victim's home as he arrives. The glare from the light above the garage door on the windshield was too much to clean up, so if the suspect did drive the victim home, there's no useable footage to ID them. Next, he runs over the forensic evidence from the victim's car. If the suspect had driven him home, there ought to be something to work with. There are no hair follicles outside of his family's, but a few fibers that don't match anything in the victim and family's closets turned up. His team has also pulled fibers from the barstool he'd occupied that night. This was interesting. The black fibers in the car didn't match anything on the stool. Therefore, the fibers were the only physical evidence left behind by the suspect. These, too, were catalogued against industry fibers and found to be about as generic as they come. Conclusion: fuck all and nothing to work with. Harlow has had his run of challenging cases, but there was always a motive. A person rarely kills just for the thrill, but he can't dismiss this possibility. The notes left behind are so vague as to suggest the suspect is just having fun at his expense. If there's no motive, there's no telling who might fall victim next. It leaves a painfully wide margin for supposition. Harlow hates speculation. It interferes with his gut. His gut has nothing to go on. It just feels sick as he returns to the 'evidence' with zero leads to act on.

The video forensics gathered from the second victim's neighborhood saw several people move past the underground residence, but only Zach was ever captured entering his dwelling that night. Peter was found on a 24-hour pawn shop's storefront camera not thirty feet from Zach's, but he'd turned and gone back the other way. Still, Harlow likes Peter for the murders, and maybe a search of his wardrobe would unearth the generic black fibers in a jogging outfit. The open window in the back alley of Zach's rental was given the complete forensics treatment, producing the shared black, generic fibers. So, he has a few minutes of video, fibers, and the cryptic notes left behind to link the killings. It's not much.

"Let's put it out to the people," his captain slides into the free chair beside his desk. She looks severe - this is always a last resort.

Harlow sighs heavily and turns to her, "it couldn't hurt," he admits, the fight leaving him.

"It's an impossible case, Will," it's not lost on Harlow that she resorts to using his first name. "What you've managed is impressive, but we've got a psycho with OCD on our hands. Even the FBI profiler suggests we reach out and inform the public."

"Is he now?" Harlow hates that it's come to this. He sees compassion enter Anderson's eyes. "Look, I know it's the right thing to do, but what do we say? There's a murderer on the loose, and to be alert? We haven't even an accurate description."

"Use the footage, show the city who to watch for. No one dresses like that in the middle of summer. That's something," Captain Anderson proposes, laying a hand on his forearm. "Have you run inquiries on the drug? The, uh, muscle relaxer."

"Yes, the Orphenadrine. No theft of the drug from any hospitals or pharmacies in the city was reported. It's a common skeletal muscle relaxant. You wouldn't believe the number of people on this stuff. Our victim's muscular injection would take full effect within 5 minutes, maybe sooner with his blood alcohol. I learned more about muscle relaxants than anyone needs to know in the past few days."

"Were you able to get names of people taking it?"

"Are you kidding me?" Harlow begged for names, but that's all confidential.

"Worth a shot," Anderson says. "Then we'll take this public, include the Orphenadrine in your release." Clever, Harlow thinks.

"So, what of your lead suspect? Peter? He's more of a nuisance having him loitering around the station."

"I guess I should release him," Harlow replies reluctantly.

"If you don't have any grounds to hold him," Anderson tells him. "Unless maybe he takes Orphenadrine? Take him home, search his place, put an officer on him if you're worried."

"I'll do that, thanks, Captain." Harlow stands, and Anderson follows. "I'll drive him back now."

"Send me your release before you put it through to PR," she lands a soft hand on his shoulder. He grunts and moves down the stairs to find Peter with a coffee in his hand, discussing Clare's disappearance with an attentive female officer.

"I'm taking you home," Harlow announces. Peter follows him, tossing the coffee in the trash.

Chapter 27

Peter feels anxious in the detective's Dodge Charger while driving from the police station to his apartment. A chemical pine scent fills his nostrils via the cardboard tree dangling from the rearview mirror. Peter finds the scent offensive and considers rolling down his window but won't assume he has that right.

"So," the detective says, his eyes on the road, "you've been making friends at the station, I hear."

Peter grumbles, "just trying to get some information on Clare's whereabouts."

"I'd tell you if I knew," Harlow replies. "It's a complicated case."

"I can't imagine why someone would abduct her," Peter's been agonizing over the news and desperate to hear something. "She's a good person."

"You believe that?"

Peter shoots a look of concern at the detective. His stern features and stiff lips pulled tight together make him seem unapproachable. He's older than Peter by about ten years, he figures, but it may just be premature lines in Harlow's face aging him. "I know she's a good person. I've known her long enough."

"But you two are on the outs; you said that yourself."

"It's not *her* fault. It was the robbery. She's not a bad person for needing space to work out her emotions. It was a traumatic scene." Peter believes this wholeheartedly, but it hurts all the same. "We were helpless. I couldn't go on the offensive with Clare in the room, and she begged me not to."

"But given the opportunity, you would have?" Harlow says almost accusingly.

"Trust me; I've been through the 'what-ifs' plenty."

"So, you would have tried to disarm the thief? Detain him?" Harlow presses. Peter doesn't like where this is going. He's trying to flesh out what level of violence he's capable of.

"I have my training," Peter admits, "but I think I used my training by being compliant."

"I agree with you," Harlow asserts. "You assessed the danger and the consequences and made an educated decision. The way you handled it was perfect."

Peter feels buoyant hearing the detective's declaration. He had handled the episode well.

"So, if you'd had the opportunity to meet up the other night as you'd planned, do you think things would have gone back to normal between you and Clare?"

Harlow says casually as if the answer wouldn't be over-analyzed.

"Yes, I believe so." Peter sinks into his seat, feeling there's nothing he can say to throw the detective off his scent. *He likes me for her vanishing.* "What is it about her disappearance that makes you say she's in danger?"

Harlow gives Peter a sideways glance. "It's going to come out tomorrow. We're releasing it to the public."

"Releasing what?" Peter likes that they're being proactive, but to put out a press release on a kidnapping seems like a last resort.

"I don't see why I shouldn't tell you," Harlow clears his throat and stops at a yellow light. "We're tracking a serial killer." He seems to let this sink in as Peter processes the information. Harlow is watching his reaction. Peter is stunned.

"Jesus, you think she's been abducted by a *serial killer?*" This news raises his anxiety level to ten. He finds he's wringing his hands in his lap. I'm not guilty of anything, he thinks, and wills himself to stop. That's just the sort of reaction the detective will be looking for.

"We've had two murders in the last couple of weeks that share a note, and that same note is what we found in your girlfriend's penthouse." Harlow creeps through the green light, buying time, Peter assumes, to have this conversation with him.

"A note? What does the note say?"

"I'm not at liberty to divulge that piece of information yet," he explains. "That it showed up at Ms. Hastings's residence is why we believe she is in danger."

Peter continues to process the news and wonders why she was abducted rather than murdered like the others. "Is it a good sign – that Clare was kidnapped and not killed outright?"

Harlow frowns as if he'd not considered this. "It's not been the killer's MO to date. We're hopeful we can locate her in time, but we've little to go on, hence the release tomorrow. We'll be counting on the public's assistance to keep an eye out for our suspect."

Peter feels lighter at the mention. "You have a suspect then?"

"We have video footage of the suspect, but not a headshot," Harlow admits. He's frustrated. A call comes in, and Harlow takes it.

"Harlow here," he says. His phone is secured to his dash on speaker.

"Detective, it's Laszlo from forensics. The video from the condo has been reviewed."

"And?" he looks to Peter, apparently indifferent over his listening in.

"We ID'd the same suspect entering the residence at 6:12 pm on the night of the abduction."

"Same dress?"

"Yes, sir," Laszlo replies. "The foyer cameras pulled little more than the hotel gave us, same with the elevators, but the connection has been made."

Harlow grumbles. "The connection was made with the notes, but I appreciate the call. Did you capture anything when the perp left with the body?" He looks at Peter.

"Yes, again, nothing we could use. They were seen leaving through the underground parking."

"Was there a vehicle?"

"No, they left through the pedestrian exit."

"No witnesses? How did the perp get her out? Was she carried out?"

"Pushed in a wheelchair the suspect brought along."

"So, they'd planned to take her," Harlow looks as if he's regretting the decision to allow Peter to listen in on the conversation now.

"From what we're seeing, yes."

"I'll be in to review the footage in an hour." Harlow hangs up and stops in front of The Bookaneer. "I'm sorry you had to hear that. It must be difficult."

"It's *something,* though," Peter feels better on some level knowing the details but helpless all the same.

"Do you mind if I come in?" the detective asks him, unlocking the car doors. Peter shrugs and gets out.

Harlow follows him. Peter takes him through the bookstore's front door and turns on the lights.

"Shouldn't you review that video?" Peter is weary as to why the detective wanted to come inside.

"I just want to perform a quick search," Harlow explains. "You could be next for all we know." He walks through the aisles of books, behind the counter, and into the office and storage rooms. He doesn't pull his weapon, so Peter assumes he still likes him for these murders. "Do you have a basement to this shop?" Peter nods and takes him to the door.

"It's not much of a basement," he offers, holding the door for the officer to descend, his hand tightening around the handle. "There's a light pull at the bottom."

Peter studies Harlow as he lumbers about the basement. Furnace, water heater, electrical board, washbasin, not much else. The basement is unfinished, as most are in these units. Just utilitarian.

Harlow returns to the top of the staircase, satisfied. "You live above the store, correct?" Peter nods again. "I should probably give it a sweep, too, if that's okay with you."

The detective's gaze lets Peter know it's not a question, and he ushers the officer up the narrow staircase and into his apartment. Harlow wears a Spartan expression as he moves through the small apartment with verve.

"Two bedrooms," he says. "Seems overkill for a single man."

"It was available, and my landlord is the store's owner," Peter explains. "Well, he's not the owner. His ex-wife is. It's a strange relationship." Why is he telling him all of this? It's his nerves acting up. He rambles when he's nervous; as when on a first date.

"So, your boss also rents you your apartment," Harlow understands. "How's that relationship?"

"Complicated," Peter admits, ready for the detective to leave. Harlow opens his closet, pushing clothing to the side.

"Okay, your space seems free of any imminent danger, though you ought to have your boss look at the wiring in the basement. Knob and tube." Harlow says conversationally as he walks to the door.

Peter follows him to the front, and Harlow promises to be in touch. Peter locks up and shuts off the lights. He returns to his apartment and readies himself for a restless night.

As expected, Peter lays in bed, glaring at the popcorn ceilings, studying their landscapes as the light from the street below casts shadows through his window. His index and third fingers press against the side of his windpipe. He feels the murmur in his chest, but fingers on the throat usually produce a calming effect. He counts heartbeats and breaths as steadily as he can muster. A pain in his side heightens his anxiety. In his exaggerated state of fight or flight, Peter picks up the slightest pinpricks and aches, creating apocalyptic scenarios.

Eventually, he overcomes the dread and succumbs to sleep. He dreams of Clare. They walk the corridor he's become familiar with under hypnosis. Clare looks at him, and in her eyes, he witnesses an infinite number of identities. He feels lost in the extraordinary depth of personalities housed within her. But he also experiences a sense of knowing, of knowing her. It is so intimate that he wakes weeping into his pillow.

Clare can't be gone. Their connection is so deep he can't process the idea she has become the third victim of this serial killer. He won't.

Chapter 28

With an unlimited ceiling to the blue skies above, Theresa lies in her manicured backyard with a lemonade in hand. Birds sing, and squirrels traverse the power lines perpendicular to the sloping fence. She loves the simplicity nature offers and its inherent ability to soothe the savage soul. Her father had created this paradise with the forethought of planting trees and shrubs and gardens so that he and her mother could enjoy the serenity of their backyard oasis in his retirement.

Now it is Theresa who benefits from her father's mindful planting. She is who maintains the yard and who would one day spend as much time as life allowed appreciating it.

Nature is something she prescribes to all her clients. Forest bathing is a term used in Japan that rings true for her. Place yourself barefoot in a forest and let nature's effect lower your blood pressure, balance your ions, cleanse your lungs and feed your soul.

She is shocked out of her reverie by the sound of a text coming through her phone. *Why did I feel the need to bring it with me?* She hesitates and then picks up the phone to view the message. It's from Peter.

Hi, Theresa, can we talk? Clare has been abducted. Peter.

Theresa senses Peter's angst. Peter's girlfriend is missing. She sits up to respond, her thumbs typing madly at her screen.

Peter, That's awful! I'm so sorry. We can talk today if you'd like. Theresa.

Peter responds immediately, asking if he can come to her home to talk. He's upset over the lives he's experienced under hypnosis. Clare had broken his heart twice before. Is that what this is? Has she left me in again?

Theresa offers a time of 5 pm, as she's planned to have lunch with Nyra and then a session with a client at 2. Peter accepts, and her day is off to a rolling start.

At lunch, Nyra explains her life in detail while Theresa listens. She is still on the fence over her marriage, the kids are acting out, and life is becoming tiresome. It's a tired tale of the bored housewife; whether that's a legitimate claim, Theresa's heard it umpteen times in sessions. Theresa checks out, nodding at appropriate moments but thinking of what her conversation will be like with Peter tonight. Peter fills her head, and she realizes a disturbing truth: she *likes* him. Like a high school crush. It's inescapable.

After lunch, she is dropped off at home to receive her client, who lives a life as a political prisoner, released and then condemned to live like a refugee. Life is hard, Theresa thinks, it's cruel and awful, but it can be beautiful and easy too. What will she tell Peter tonight to give him that sense of wonder now that Clare has disappeared?

Peter arrives five minutes early as the buses run on time tonight. Theresa welcomes him and leads Peter to the kitchen, where she has a charcuterie board laid out and a bottle of wine open.

"I didn't know if you'd had a chance to eat, so I laid out a few things." Peter looks a bit disoriented. "This is a personal visit, Peter, one friend meeting with another." She picks up a glass and offers it to Peter. He takes it reluctantly, and she pours a 5-ounce glass of the chardonnay. "I like a white in the summer months, don't you?" Small talk has never been her forte, but she's trying.

Peter nods, his expression blank. He wasn't expecting this to be so informal, Theresa realizes. Maybe she shouldn't have been so forward.

"I - thank you for this, I'm not very hungry, but the wine might help," he smiles out of the side of his face, eyes locking with hers for a moment, and Theresa feels a connection.

"You said Clare has been abducted," Theresa decides to skip the small talk and charge ahead with the topic top of mind. "What happened?"

"I'm being told she was abducted from her apartment and is in danger. Her mother alerted the police, and they found the place in disarray and Clare missing." Theresa notices how Peter is short of breath after his explanation.

"That's awful, Peter; I'm so sorry," Theresa touches his forearm delicately. "What's being done about it?"

"Yeah, so I've been revisited by that detective, the one who questioned Clare and me on the murder of our robber," Peter takes a sip of the fruity wine. "So, yesterday he came with the news of Clare missing and a note and had me come to the station for what he called 'my own good,' but I know he's thinking I'm the one who has Clare and that I'm a serial murderer and -" Peter stops to fill his lungs with a shaky breath.

Theresa squeezes Peter's forearm now, resting on the kitchen island. "Please, breathe, Peter. I'm listening."

Peter inhales deeply and exhales slowly. He does this twice more. "I'm sorry, I just felt I needed to see you on this. To vent, I guess. I'm rattled. I don't know what to do. I feel helpless."

"That's all very understandable," Theresa says in a whisper. "But if you haven't done these things, don't waste your energy worrying about being blamed for it."

"You don't think I've done them?" Peter's expression falls.

"Oh, no, Peter, I know you haven't done them. You aren't the type." She picks up a grape from the board and slips it in her mouth, perhaps too sensually. It bursts perfectly, pairing nicely with the wine.

Peter starts to pace, the chardonnay swishing in the glass. "I feel like I need to see her, you know. I want to hold her."

Theresa feels a stab of jealousy. *Why? Because taking Peter in like this isn't professional, and neither are your feelings toward him.* "I'm sure she would take great comfort in that, Peter."

"The past lives, I don't care about them. I want to be with her regardless. I want to take the chance. If my heart gets broken, that's on me." He's become animated, and some of the wine leaps out of his glass, landing on the island and splashing them both.

Theresa rushes to pull a dishcloth from the counter and wipes away the puddle. She takes Peter's arm and dries it as well. He seems vulnerable and preoccupied.

"It's brave, what you're saying, Peter," she assures him. "And I'm sure you'll have that opportunity to see her again. If a murderer absconds with a person rather than murders them, then there's a chance."

"That's what Detective Harlow thinks. That maybe they'll find her before long." He leans the palms of his hands against the marble top of the island, his head falling forward.

Harlow, Theresa recalls the name. It sparks a chill in her to remember the part a detective with the same name had played in her young life. Harlow was the detective's name who had responded to her case – her parent's case after they were murdered in her own home. She had been away at school but was first on the scene, returning to the horror of finding her parents lying together on the dining room floor. Blood had soaked the carpet. Their bodies were cold when she rushed to shake them awake. The scent that had assailed her upon the discovery assaults her memories, and she crosses her arms across her chest, rubbing her palms along her exposed shoulders.

She waves off the feeling of dread and tells herself to step out of the past and into the present. It's a complex memory to pull away from, but she is practiced in the methodology. 2011 was the year her life had changed forever. She had only survived by transforming her life. She is a survivor; she reminds herself.

"*Harlow*, the name sounds familiar," she says ironically. "What's his first name?"

"Oh, I don't know," Peter seems caught off-guard by the question, raises his head, and picks up his glass, tilting it into his mouth and draining its contents. He breaths deeply and pushes off the island. "I'm feeling useless," he tells her, hands rubbing at his face.

"You can help by telling the police what you know, Peter. That's how you can feel useful. Don't fall prey to the 'what-ifs.' That serves no one."

Peter concurs with a weak grunt and nods. Theresa pours him more wine. He drinks this too quickly, as well. She senses he doesn't want to be here and is rushing through their time together. This makes Theresa feel uncomfortable, and she suggests they go to her treatment room.

"It's okay, I'm okay," Peter sounds like he's convincing himself. "I'm just consumed by what Harlow told me. I don't know how to express what I'm feeling."

"This is clearly affecting you negatively, and you're experiencing triggers," Theresa explains. "You feel guilty over something you have no control over."

Peter stops pacing and looks at Theresa. "That's it," he points a finger at her from under his stemmed glass. "I feel guilty."

"But *why*, Peter?" Theresa is going to take a different approach, she's decided.

Peter takes a moment to collect his thoughts. "I've been a part of her life the past couple of weeks," his eyes dart back and forth as if struggling with the answer. "She experienced the robbery with me – at *my* place. She backed off. I'm guilty of something there."

Theresa looks kindly at Peter, head tilting. "You're no more guilty of Clare's disappearance than the chaos the suicide bomber set in motion while you served in Afghanistan."

"I don't believe that. I don't know if I believe that," Peter says hurriedly, his head shaking, supporting himself with both hands pressed into the island countertop.

"You're looking for something that isn't there." She tells him quietly. "Why? Why do you need to feel responsible? What's making you take on so much?" She rounds the island, and they are a foot apart. Peter looks at her, and Theresa's heart leaps a moment as he remains tied to her gaze. She places her free hand on his upper arm and squeezes just enough that he knows she's here for him. She swallows and nearly closes her eyes but stops herself from leaning in to kiss away his grief.

Peter seems to sense the potentially awkward moment and takes a step back. Theresa comes to her senses, pushing up her glasses and snapping out a suggestion.

"Let's meet in a few days, Peter. We'll run another session. Perhaps there will be something there you can use."

Peter goes to pull his phone from his pocket. "Shit, I left my phone at home," he says. "Can you write the day and time down for me? I'm forgetting everything right now."

"Sure," Theresa walks to her office, grabs a sheet of printer paper, and jots down the time, handing Peter the sheet.

"Thank you," he says meekly, bending the thick stock and placing it in his pocket. "I'd better get back; I should be by my phone."

"Of course," Theresa says, walking him out. She hates to see him go, thinking she hasn't been much help, but sometimes a listening ear is enough. She won't push her luck with him. It was stupid for her to have leaned into Peter like that. He's vulnerable. He's missing his girlfriend. She was taking advantage.

After Peter is gone, Theresa fills her glass and enters the dining room - now sitting room, where her parent's met their untimely end. She places her glass down on a side table as memories assault her - the unlocked door, the silence, and the shock of discovering her parent's bodies. The shock is enough to spark the

PTSD she's worked so hard to bury as she relives the scene.

She practices her breathing and sits upright, her hands clenched together. She was robbed of her parents at a difficult age. She was in college, figuring herself out. Now she wonders what her life would have been like if they'd survived. Would she have gone off to study regression therapy? Would her life resemble the solitary one it's become? Would she be a different person? These and other questions have tormented her since the moment she'd landed on the gruesome discovery. How do I go on? How do I fix this? Can this be fixed? Can I be fixed?

Psychologists and her decision to branch off into regression therapy answered some of these questions. Now she helps others through their difficult periods. She provides others the gift of past lives to draw from, as she had.

Theresa relaxes into the comfortable chair, crosses her legs into the lotus position, and decides to meditate on this, revisiting her own past lives and the lessons they'll offer to further justify her choices. After several minutes, she switches gears and uses future life progression techniques to understand what is forecast. She's careful not to do so often, as it feels like crossing a boundary perilously close to black magic. The future isn't set in stone, but aspects of it can carry through all possible timelines. What she learns only serves to distress her.

Chapter 29

Peter feels weak with fear for Clare. That detective has it in for me, he thinks. Even if the surveillance cameras show I hadn't entered the robber's home to kill him, he likes me for the murder. He likes me for Clare's disappearance. It's all too much. Peter feels the rise of anxiety grip his chest, and a growing warmth scorch the surface of his cheeks.

"Probable or possible," he repeats to himself, unboxing books and arranging them on his shelves. It can't be probable that they'll pin the crimes on him. He didn't do them. They may try, but where's the proof? This line of thought eases the effects of the panic attack.

He consults his phone and sees that the local news is rerunning Clare's disappearance. Good, he thinks. The more eyes on the evidence Harlow offered, the better the chances. *Where on earth is she?*

"We're asking for information from the public on the disappearance of Clare Hastings. You're seeing the video footage of our suspect dressed in a black, baggy tracksuit and last seen in Grand Forks. The victim was a resident of Detroit, as were the others. If you've seen our suspect or anyone resembling the video description, please call the number below," Harlow says to the cameras. The video shows a high-angle shot of a robust-looking, potentially homeless person dressed all in black on a split-screen. "Our suspect has remained just out of reach but know we're doing everything in our power to bring Clare Hastings home safely. We believe she is the third person affected by this individual over the past fourteen days. We have collected evidence from each scene that confirms we have a serial murderer in our city. They are not particular when choosing their victim. Sex, age, profession, religion, none of these are shared attributes among the victims. None are related in any way. Be diligent, be safe." Clare's photo fills Peter's screen next. "If you've seen Clare Hastings, please call us immediately. If you have any information concerning Clare's disappearance, please call. She was last seen entering her home at 12:37 pm on June 21st. The address is listed in the information on your screen. We thank you for your cooperation."

Harlow didn't mention the note that links the victims, Peter notices. He's keeping that information from the public. *Why?* He's also kept the identities of the other two victims anonymous. How much longer could he keep that information from the media? Peter realizes it's been three days since he saw Theresa and longer since he's heard anything more about Clare's disappearance.

He pulls a sheet of paper from his pocket. It's the date and time of his next session with Theresa, hand-written on her stationery. He unfolds it and lays it on the counter by the register. "I need to do some laundry," he tells himself. He'd forgotten he'd pocketed the note and, apparently, about doing laundry this week. He already added the time into his phone calendar as Theresa had texted him it as well – just in case. The session is for tomorrow. Theresa mentioned it was to review their findings and then develop a treatment. Before he can move the note to the blue bin, he spins around at the sound of the door opening.

His heart doesn't know whether to leap or plummet as his eyes fall on Detective Harlow. Peter feels stuck in place, waiting for whatever news the detective has brought him. *Has he come to arrest me now?*

"Sorry to barge in like this," Harlow announces, "A nagging detail kept me up last night, and I wanted to run it past you."

"Is there no news?" Peter feels disheartened he's come only to ask more questions.

"Nothing I can share with the public," Harlow replies. "So, no news is good news, right?"

Peter will assume that's right. "What's on your mind?"

Harlow scratches his growing bald spot and seems to consider his question carefully. Peter watches him roll it around in his head.

"Your PTSD, it's uh, from your role as a peacekeeper?"

"That's one train of thought," Peter replies, curious as to why it's come up.

"But you have attended Group and claim to suffer its effects." Harlow has done his research.

"I *do* suffer its effects, Detective," Peter assures him.

"So, you move out here to get away from your home life? Why didn't you stay with your parents and get better? Why move out here?"

"My mother has enough to deal with. My father has dementia. I didn't want to be a burden."

"So, why Detroit? Why come to my city?"

"Is this *your* city?" Peter suddenly feels defensive.

Harlow laughs at this, "well, I've lived here all my life. I guess I'm territorial that way." He paces around the high-backed chairs, smoothing a palm over the worn leather top.

"Trust me; if I had any idea I'd be considered a serial murderer, I'd have chosen differently."

Harlow and Peter share a look of defiance. Harlow's expression softens while Peter feels his harden. Harlow must have noticed him become flush.

"You haven't been to Group in weeks," the detective states. "They've been worried. You know how they get."

"So, you're here on behalf of the Veteran Support Group?" Peter feels like he's being watched. He doesn't appreciate Harlow asking around about him like this.

Harlow barks out another laugh. "Nah, they just want to know you're alright. I filled them in on the finer details." He pulls a pad and pen from his deep, coat pocket. "Are you seeing anyone about your PTSD now?"

"Is that anyone's business but mine?"

"I'm just doing my job, Peter," Harlow had never called him by his first name before. He must want this information.

"Yes," Peter offers, "I'm seeing someone. I have it under control." He feels his face cooling down and his heart rate slow.

"I know the whole doctor/patient privilege act won't get me far, but can you share who you're seeing with me?" He asks with a pen at the ready.

Peter considers telling him, but he'd had a candid conversation with Theresa over wine that she could be convinced to share with Harlow. Would she? Fuck it, he thinks. "To cooperate with your investigation and return Clare, I'll give it to you."

Peter slides the stationary Theresa had given him off the counter and hands it to Harlow. The detective returns his pen and pad to study the document.

Harlow holds it up in front of him and seems stunned for a moment. "This is very helpful. I appreciate you not holding out on me."

Peter squints as if confused over its importance and shrugs, "I only want to see Clare safe and sound, Detective. Even if you still doubt that, I hope you're looking at suspects other than me."

Harlow looks almost chastened, which makes Peter optimistic. "Look, Peter, I get that you're honestly worried about your girlfriend. I'm sorry if I've seemed difficult. You've been very open about your comings and goings and your relationship with the victim. It's all appreciated."

"Do you have other suspects?" Peter feels he must ask again.

"I can't comment on that, but open collaboration is important. As I said in the news release, we're doing everything we can to bring her back." He waves the paper again and thanks Peter for his support.

Peter watches him leave. "Take care of yourself, Peter," he says, and the bell rings over the door.

Peter sits heavily in one of the high-backed chairs in front of the electric fireplace. *Are they really investigating anyone other than me?*

Harlow sits in his car just a few yards from The Bookaneer, looking at the piece of paper in his hands. The name on the stationary reads Theresa Clement, Regression Therapist. He'd been stunned to read it in front of Peter. The name rang a bell. It rang and rang and rang as he processed it. *Clement*: it's the couple's name murdered in their home all those years ago. His first lead case. The one that had gone sideways when the meth heads who'd murdered them were themselves found beaten to death. What was the daughter's name again? The details escape him now. He would return to the office and review the case notes.

Harlow radios in and asks Admin to pull the file. Somethings got his guts churning. He feels the weight of the paper and pulls out into the street, his tires squealing.

Chapter 30

As Theresa adds her handwritten notes from Peter's sessions to her computer, the lessons emerging from his lives become clearer.

A man doomed to suffer a lynching, another who died by beheading, and two lives where he'd had his heart broken. Hearts are broken daily, but, in Theresa's experiences, violent deaths aren't as common as some might think. Peter had suffered through tumultuous times in both lives, ending in sadistic and frightening deaths. That sort of trauma leaves a scar that traverses many lives. It is cataloged and retrieved from the Akashic records, accessed through the unconscious mind. It acts like genetic memory: wherein memories are incorporated into the genome, inherited through ancestral experiences over long periods. With the Akashic records, the soul's memory is being accessed.

Both times he'd represented the meek who suffered executions at the hands of the ruling class, his hands bound and feeling helpless. These experiences could explain his PTSD as they surfaced during his real-world encounter in Afghanistan. All three traumatic events left him feeling vulnerable and helpless to prevent them. This sense of helplessness is the key to Peter's healing. He felt powerless to protect those children at the airport. He was defenseless to prevent either of his brutal deaths.

His heartbreaking tales also play a role in his current life by showing him that love and relationships aren't as simple as they seem. Bringing two people together is one thing but keeping them together involves navigating many more factors and outside influences than just the two of you. That he was powerless to stop his husband from cheating on him and Feliks's change of heart also speaks to Peter's vulnerabilities. That Clare has twice broken his heart doesn't bode well for a future with her. Their shared event with the armed robbery already shows signs of the dissolution of their relationship. Still, Peter explained his desire to pursue Clare. Theresa doesn't want to see him suffer a repeat of this pairing. She likes Peter far too much to see him in pain.

Peter will be at her door in a few minutes, and she will review her findings with him. She will present opportunities to correct his life by overcoming his feelings of helplessness and misplaced guilt. His trauma in Afghanistan has forced his past lives to resurface, and his relationship with Clare seems to have shifted from an equal standing to his being the underdog once more.

Peter rings her doorbell, and Theresa greets him with a more personal touch. She hugs him, and he hugs her back. He looks disheveled. His hair is unkempt, as though he'd been running his hands through it absently on his commute. He has dark bags under his eyes, and his short-sleeved shirt is buttoned incorrectly, the top button hanging loosely where it ought to be secured and the bottom of his shirt untucked. This is not how Theresa has come to know Peter. He has always presented well.

"Oh, Peter," Theresa says, ushering him in. "You don't look yourself today."

Peter grunts his consensus, looking down at where Theresa's focus remains. He quickly unbuttons and rebuttons his shirt. "It's been a week," he admits.

"Has there been any news about Clare's disappearance?"

Peter shakes his head and sits. This is not a regression session, Theresa had explained. This is a summary of his past lives to prioritize treatment. They remain in the sitting room.

Theresa relates her findings, and Peter seems even more detached from the present. She doesn't want Peter to distance himself from the work, and she would hate to think he blames her for the discoveries. His aura has returned to a state similar to their initial meeting, isolated and separated from the world.

"Peter," she leans forward in her chair and touches his knee as he wrings his hands. "This information is a gift; it will help you overcome your PTSD. Now that we have the root causes and can see the connections in all three lives, the work can truly begin. What do we know? You couldn't stop the lynching, you couldn't prevent the beheading, and you were following orders when those children died. At no time were you to blame."

"I get it," Peter replies, head down, forearms resting on his thighs, hands building friction. "Still, I feel responsible."

"You were helpless to do anything more than you had in all three scenarios," Theresa reinforces. "It's that helplessness you felt, you still feel, that we need to work on. And the guilt that accompanies your PTSD in this life."

"I do feel helpless. Especially now," his sad eyes look up at Theresa, and desperation penetrates her. "I need Clare to be found. I need her to be okay."

Theresa changes her tactics to put Peter back on track. "I want you to focus on the PTSD, Peter." Theresa pulls back and references her notes. "It's true that Clare's influence in your life has left you feeling helpless as well. This is a recurring issue in your lives. But the main cause of your PTSD are the other two events, and Afghanistan was the precursor in the present. I want to rid you of this karmic event so you don't suffer it again."

"Clare is *missing*," Peter announces. "It's all I can think about." He pushes off his thighs and sits up straight. Theresa flinches. "How do I work on *myself* when I can only think of her?"

"Peter, what happens if they find Clare's body?" Theresa surprises herself by asking this.

Peter stares at her for a long moment and sits heavily on the sofa. "I'd be devastated," he insists.

"Then you must distance yourself from Clare and the 'what-ifs' and refocus on why you came to me in the first place." His preoccupation with Clare angers her.

"But this is happening to me *now*, not a year ago or two-hundred years ago; how can I put any energy into anything other than Clare's safe return?" Peter is becoming disagreeable.

"You have no *control* over the outcome, Peter," Theresa says abruptly. "You can only *react* to her abduction, and your reaction should be mindful. You have no power to change what's happening. Leave that to the police."

"Powerless," Peter says, despondent.

"Yes," Theresa lets that sink in. "Like I said, a recurring theme for you. To get past this feeling, you need to do the *work*, and focusing on Clare's whereabouts isn't going to help you."

Peter nods slowly. "I understand," he says, the words catching in his throat, his hands rising to his face. He shudders and cries.

Theresa feels awful for him but needs him to truly understand that the work they've accomplished is important, and he must now accept what they've learned and do the work to move past it.

"You don't have to feel helpless, Peter. You don't have to feel guilty. You're a strong person with a good heart who has his whole life ahead of him. You will learn to feel empowered. We will work together on that."

"I'm sorry," Peter tells her, standing. "I don't know if I can do the work right now," he turns to the door and opens it. Stopping at the threshold, Theresa thinks he may turn around, but he doesn't.

She follows him to the front door and remains standing at the threshold. It's a warm evening with a light breeze picking up grass clippings from her neighbor's yard. She watches Peter leave, walk down her driveway, and studies him until he disappears around a heavily treed corner.

Chapter 31

Harlow is desperate with two dead, one missing, and only the generic fabric, the killer's calling card, and Peter connecting the last two. The thing about Peter is he doesn't exhibit defensive behavior analogous to a guilty person. People tend to go on the defensive when they have something to hide. Rather, Peter has been an open book. That could mean he's a psychopath, and a pathological liar, lacking remorse or shame, but Harlow hasn't read that in his personality or how he carries himself. Harlow's worked cases like that before.

He stares at the board in front of him, where the Karma Killer's victims stare pleadingly back. There's a connection. *You just have to find it.* He runs his hands through his dark, thinning hair and scratches his scalp roughly. His coffee is cold, and his leads more so. He'd found nothing inside Peter's bookstore or apartment to suggest he was hiding a body, wearing clothing that matched the killer's outfit, or using the muscle relaxant. An officer has been stationed outside The Bookaneer to watch him, and no suspicious movements have been reported. To propose the killer is selecting random people seems purposeless. Serial killers want to believe they're killing for a reason, but to date, no breadcrumbs are leading them in that direction.

Karma has a Champion. They deserved it. Signed: *The Karma Killer.* That's all the notes left with the bodies ever revealed. Very few people, in Harlow's opinion, deserved to die. And to die in the bizarre ways these two victims had added to his confusion. There was no consistency there either. One hanged by the neck. One with his head removed and placed on his lap. Now a missing person with only the note to study. He fears for Ms. Hastings. What's the MO? *Karma.* Okay, so they believe the victims deserved what they got, but why? He'd love to sit down with this serial murderer and pick their brain. Even the FBI profilers are stumped. They can't say if it's a man or a woman, but history favors a man. The brevity of the notes left behind speak of someone very focused who needs no one's approval but want's the world to know they've paid a karmic debt. Then is it about revenge? Revenge could mean so many things. None of the victims went to the same schools. None worked in the same company. Social circles spanned one end of the spectrum to the other. The FBI figures a white man for the murders, as most serial killers are. So, this is little help. They'd managed height from the surveillance, the perp's gait didn't give up much because of the heavy outfit, and weight was also difficult to discern. Still, they've made a profile.

Items found on the bodies – save the notes, do not attempt to link them to each other, so that's been a dead end. That they all live in Detroit is a long shot. *What else do they have in common?* Harlow pulls up the credit card and bank statements for each again to revisit where they shopped for their groceries, their clothing, and baubles. Each one is different. No overlap. Has the killer witnessed a theft and then delivered their brand of punishment? It seems excessive for the crime, though that was Zach's last act.

Harlow's placed undercover in the stores mentioned for the past two weeks to assess the customers. Many have been interviewed, but all had solid alibis.

A red string connects each identity from thumbtacks terminating on a map where the bodies were found. Communities, religions, and finances all vary. This killer is not favoring the rich over the poor or spiritual beliefs. The victims are two men and one woman, so the person's sex doesn't play into it. There were no signs of sexual assault.

How many more karmic debts would be paid before he caught the Karma Killer? Two of the victims were decent people from all outward appearances. Their search histories cataloged on their devices confirmed this. Not even a visit to a porn site. No secret chats or dating site creepers. Nothing. *So, what's the connection. Karma isn't enough to go on, not by a mile.* This is a real curveball, and it is getting old. Not unlike his first investigation into the murders of the Clement couple has he had reporters breathing down his neck like this. *The Clements.* He's reviewed their case again. The daughter *was* named Theresa. He's checked her priors, and she's clean. She remains in her familial home, running her business out of it. Still, he's sent the stationary Peter presented him to forensics for comparisons to the stock and ink used in the Karma Killer's notes on a hunch. He figures a long shot, but his gut's telling him something else.

He mouses his cursor over his email and erases multiple queries from journalists digging for more. He has nothing more to give them. He can't give them what little he has - the notes - or the killer may disappear. He hates that he's waiting on another murder. But maybe the killer will slip up and offer a clue he can work with. He hates everything about this investigation and feels the failure of that first case nagging at him. *Is this the perfect crime?*

His phone rings, and he answers. Another reporter. They're following the case closely. The public needed to be alerted to a possible serial killer in their midst. It was the right thing to do, and putting out the video surveillance and Clare's headshot was an excellent place to start. The public has a general idea now of what the perp wears, and they've already received dozens of calls. Still, Harlow hasn't given them much, not even the name connected to the killings. Christ, that would be sensationalized in the media. *The Karma Killer?* They would eat that up. He explains to the reporter that the police and FBI are doing everything to identify and arrest the murderer. He tells her they have questioned dozens of potential suspects, and anonymous tips are being followed up. He gives the woman just enough and hangs up.

It's late, and he strolls through the mostly empty station. He catches the eye of one of the support staff screening tips through the glass of the call center. They nod at one another. The FBI agent has left for the day; Harlow notices that the man's desktop computer is running screen savers of the crime scenes. It's a morbid collection, but he understands the need to be connected to the crimes. He's dreamed about them, scenarios running through his head non-stop.

He makes his way to the forensics lab to enquire about the stationary, but they've asked him for another 12 hours to complete their analysis. They seem pretty backed up.

Theresa Clement, he thinks. She was distraught over her parents' deaths, understandably, and she had lashed out at him. He considers paying her a visit. She may not discuss Peter's case, but maybe her assessment of his current state of mind will help. He will arrange an appointment with her.

He turns around and heads back to his desk. He punches in Theresa's webpage address and reviews it. She deals with past life regression. Harlow researches this on a separate tab. Seems like a fraudulent business to him, like a psychic medium or fortune teller. Upon further reading, he learns that regression therapy puts a person in a trance-like state to relive their 'past lives.' *Nonsense.* Harlow finds the contact page. Here he punches in a pseudonym and creates a life story that is not his own. He leaves his cell phone as his contact. If she doesn't get back to him in the next few hours, he'll just show up tomorrow morning.

Chapter 32

Clare is weak. She's also freezing. Had it been a day? *Days?* Gagged and desperate, she is beginning to feel hopeless over a possible rescue. There are tens of thousands of basements in Detroit, and she can't even say whether she's still in the city.

Light penetrates the darkness as the door atop the stairs opens. Could this be the police? Have they found her? No. The figure is the same as before. Heavily clad in what looks like three layers of tracksuits. Nothing is said. The silence makes way for the footfalls as they navigate the squeaky staircase.

Clare struggles weakly against her restraints and grumbles to let her go. Tears wet the rag tied around her face, forcing her jaw open. She's never been so uncomfortable, and she's never been so terrified. Warm urine soaks her light pants. It stings. She's so dehydrated. There's not much pee, but she remembers hearing that a potential rapist would be put off if you wet yourself. If this should be her fate, she hopes the advice is accurate.

But this seems different than that. There has been no attempt to touch her, never mind sexually. Her captor seems content to feed her vinegar from a distance and simply keep her as a neglected pet.

The rag gagging her is removed, and a new rag damp with vinegar hovers in front of her face. She thirstily places her dry lips around it and pulls the liquid in. Her tongue retreats and lips sting to life, and she wants to spit but can't summon the saliva.

"Water," she begs in a gravelly voice. "Please,"

The figure pauses and then moves laboriously to a laundry tub and pours water onto the rag. Clare wonders whether they move slowly because of the layers of clothing or for effect. She wants to scream out, but her throat and mouth are so dry she doubts she could manage a squeak. The rag is presented to her, and she sucks at it. This time the water satisfies an inkling of her thirst. Her stomach grumbles angrily. She's impossibly hungry, having no idea how long she's been here.

"Thank you," Clare says, her throat no longer feeling as if coated in sand. "Why -"

Clare's question is cut off as her captor replaces the original rag in her mouth. Clare bounces in the chair, screeching in frustration, moving her head side to side to prevent the rag's return. She is unsuccessful. She grunts her disapproval, but these fall on deaf ears. The figure sits in a chair opposite her and stares.

Does this person know me? Clare is running out of possibilities. To keep a person alive in a basement seems like a terrible fate where she will eventually starve to death. *What in the hell is this person's game? Is it a game?* Can she win it?

Perhaps that this person hasn't revealed their identity is a good thing. Maybe this is just a scare tactic.

But to what end? There is nothing she can think of that could – wait, is this *karma* being visited upon her? She has no memory of past lives where she tormented another soul like this. Still, there seems to be no other reason she can think of; karma might be the only explanation that makes sense.

Clare thinks there is nothing I can do to stop whatever this person is planning if this is the case. I'm utterly helpless.

Chapter 33

Morning is announced with a song interrupting Harlow's dream. He remembers snippets of it as he pushes himself up on his elbows. There was a river. Impassable. It was raining. He feels a sense of dread and picks up his cell phone, canceling the alarm. I've ruined that song for myself now, he muses. It's 6:45 am, and he checks his texts.

One text catches his eye: *Unknown.* He opens the message and reads it. It's Theresa Clement, Regression Therapist. She would like to see him in an initial session to discuss his history and develop a plan. Three dates are offered, one being today at 12:30 pm. He responds immediately to fill the appointment.

Harlow showers and decides he's no time to shave. He picks up breakfast at a drive-through and demolishes a bacon and egg bagel on the way to the station. The coffee is too hot to drink right away.

He checks in with the forensics lab at the station, and they mention his results for the stationary are on his desk. He sprints up the stairs and finds the envelope containing the information. He pauses before opening it, his gut telling him it will match the stock of the notes left by the Karma Killer.

He's right; both the stock and the ink used to print the header are a match. What does this mean? It means he has something to go on. Finally. What to do next? He doesn't want to spook her. He decides to wait until his appointment to approach Theresa. He feels he owes her that much. To call in the calvary now seems presumptuous of him. He would hate to be wrong about her and have this become an embarrassment. *Would she remember him?* He's aged, he admits. His face is drawn down in a frown most of the time. He's lost some hair, and he's unshaven. He's 11 years older. He can probably pull this off.

Besides, it would be a rookie move to announce it before he could get a read on Theresa. If she's the Karma Killer, she has Clare Hastings right now. If they rush in, she might kill her if she hasn't already. But there's no indication that she has yet. It's a Schrodinger's Cat scenario: Clare is both alive and dead, locked away somewhere. He'd be much happier to find her alive.

Harlow feels the adrenaline calling him to arms, but he's smarter than to react to an impulse. He's experienced. He's not going to fuck this up. He'll take it slow, but not too slow. He'll keep this information to himself until he's had a chance to feel her out.

He decides to call Peter. It's only 7:45 am but Peter answers.

"It's Detective Harlow," he announces. "Do you have a session with Theresa Clement today?"

"Uh, no, not until next week," Peter replies; he sounds anxious. "Why?"

"Just part of the ongoing investigation, nothing to worry about." Harlow wonders if he sounds convincing on the other end.

"Detective, I - what are you not telling me?"

Then something dawns on Harlow. The second murder victim was connected, albeit briefly, to Peter. The missing person is also connected to Peter. It's why Harlow liked Peter for the Karma Killer. But what about the first victim? He wasn't linked to Peter, but the question was never really put to him.

"Peter, do you know a Mr. Sanderson? Fred Sanderson?"

"He's my boss, Detective," a pause, "what's happened?" Peter sounds a little shaken.

"Your boss!" This information forces Harlow back in his chair, the declaration flooring him. If this is the same man, then all three victims are attached to Peter.

"He owns the bookstore?"

"No, his ex-wife does. She's remarried, though. Name's Balthazar. Sanderson runs it. It's his pet project. He hired me, but she pays me."

This is why Harlow hadn't learned of the business. It's not in his name. He checks his notepad, and sure enough, Peter had relayed that information to him days before. Sanderson was an entrepreneur with several dealings, but books weren't one Harlow had been made aware of.

"Peter," Harlow's tone becomes desperate. "When was the last time you saw Fred Sanderson?"

"Um, a couple of weeks ago. He doesn't frequent the store." Peter's voice is hollow. "What's happened?"

Harlow snaps the photo of Sanderson he has on the board, sending it to Peter's phone. "I just sent you a photo. Please confirm this is your boss."

After a moment of silence, Peter returns with a yes. "That's him. What's going on, Detective?" Peter sounds frazzled now.

"You haven't seen him in two weeks because he became the first victim of our serial murderer two weeks ago." Harlow's gut has cleared Peter of the crimes. Next, he will dig deeper.

"What? H - he's dead?"

"Yes, very much so. Hanged, in fact. We didn't release information on how the victims died, but he was hanged. As you know, the second victim was beheaded. The third is missing."

"Detective," Peter says, clearly roused from the information. "Do you know where Clare is?"

"I think I do," Harlow replies.

"I think I do too."

"Say it," Harlow asks of Peter. "Theresa Clement," Peter responds.

"Sit tight, Peter. I'll have an officer pick you up at The Bookaneer in a minute." He hangs up and requests the pickup from the officer assigned to watch Peter.

It's early, but Harlow still wants to confront Theresa himself before involving the FBI. He decides to go to her home alone and wait.

Chapter 34

Rain falls sideways on the front lawn as Theresa studies how the westward winds push her fifty-year-old blue spruce as if it were a reed. She's feeling melancholy today, reflecting on the work performed over the past two weeks with Peter. She wonders over the dynamics of the relationship she and Peter have formed. A plan going forward to treat his PTSD through what they've learned has been penned, and she feels a shock of excitement as she reflects on their next session, hoping it will go her way.

With Clare out of the picture, she stands a chance at seeing where they can take the intimate knowledge collected to become closer. It's not professional, but she's in a position now to see if Peter is receptive to the idea of making their relationship personal.

She stands to approach the front picture window, where the storm has lessened now to a drizzle. Summer storms, she thinks, are unpredictable. People, not so much. Karma commands their will. No karmic debt ever goes unpaid. People create their own. Like Clare. Like Sanderson and that deadbeat who robbed Peter's store.

Clare wouldn't have changed. She would break Peter's heart just as surely as Sanderson would have continued to spike his PTSD. Clare, locked in Theresa's basement, can do no more damage to Peter. She will die there. She will die, never knowing why this fate has befallen her, but it will make sense during her intermission between lives. When people can't realize they're repeating the same damaging behavior time and again, they need to be taught the lesson they aren't learning. Theresa is that teacher. Leaving notes with each act gave her a voice. It told the world that karma is inescapable. As the Karma Killer, Clare stood outside herself. The meek woman born of her parent's murders receded, and her alter-ego stepped up to the plate. The Karma Killer, too, was fashioned from grief.

So, why did she take Clare and not finish her off in the penthouse? It's karma. The heart will fail first during starvation if she does it right. In essence, Clare's heart will be broken. In the basement, she's given no food and little water. Then, once weak to the point of expiring, Theresa will take the body to the woods. That shouldn't take more than a week, and a week is nearly up.

The sun breaks through the dark sky, and Theresa notices a car across the street. She doesn't recognize it, but that's no reason to be spooked. Still, a sense of foreboding enters her chest. She squints against the light and sees a man sitting quietly in the driver's seat of a Dodge Charger.

The rain returns with a vengeance, blurring the car and the man inside. She will take a new client on at 12:30, but it's only 9 am. This couldn't be him, could it? Unlikely. Then an image forms in her mind. A man she'd not seen in many years but whose name Peter had uttered. Detective Harlow!

Theresa breaks into a cold sweat. It was only a moment she'd laid eyes on the man in the car, but that's all it took. Memories rush in of his initial visit, where he took her aside and questioned her on the discovery of her parents. He was kind, young, and ruggedly handsome. Then, as the investigation dragged on, Theresa became despondent. She went to psychiatrists and counselors and then discovered regression therapy. It took one session with the regressionist to offer her the identities of her parent's murderers. She spent every waking hour looking for them. Going on the police's initial assumptions, Theresa looked in the poorest communities in Detroit for a pair of junkies. She became obsessed with finding them. She dressed in dark, baggy clothes, searching the impoverished areas of her city. She visited soup kitchens and even stayed in homeless shelters. For everyone she met, she held their gaze. She was looking for the window that would reveal the identity of her parent's murderers.

Eventually, she found one. Rage made a home where diligence had lived. It had been weeks. She felt homeless herself. She had lost weight, taken up smoking, and began drinking from shared bottles around garbage-can fires. She had fully committed to that life to see justice served.

Before acting out her murderous rage, she knew this man would lead her to the second, and sure enough, Theresa's patience paid off. On an especially dark night, in an alley where the two sat to inject the heroin Theresa had bought for them, she played out her vengeance. It was brutal. The brick she'd picked up crumbled upon impact over the taller, more malicious-looking monster's head. He arched forward, the needle still securely in his vein. The second looked up with a toothless smile as if what she'd done were funny. His eyes were glossed over, and he was giggling like an idiot. Theresa picked up another discarded brick and slammed it into his dark, cruel face. His thin skin split, and blood gushed. He attempted a howl, but she stepped on his throat. He tried feebly to fight her off, but Theresa put all her weight behind her foot, crushing his windpipe.

The dazed junkie regained consciousness, trying to stand, but didn't make it to his knees before Theresa kicked him down. He fell to the ground slowly, so she continued to stomp on his head until blood puddled beneath it.

Not to mistake them for dead, she stood on their chests until a satisfying snap emerged from both. Then, in a fit of genius, Theresa arranged their bodies as she'd remembered her parent's lifeless forms on the dining room floor.

She signed up to go away for regression training the next day and was gone within the week. But not before Detective Harlow came with the good news. Her parent's killers were dead. Then he'd dared to ask Theresa her whereabouts the night the killers had died.

She raised hell for that, and Harlow never revisited the accusation. Besides, she'd had an alibi. She had bought a ticket for the movies on the other end of town before returning to her junkies, who'd agreed to take her up on the free heroin. The theatre she'd chosen included an exit to the right of the screen where she'd taped the latch open so she could sneak back in after the killings. This ensured that she was captured entering and leaving the theatre on their security camera. That, paired with her outrage over the questioning, put the case to bed.

She revels in the memory of her vigilantism but never killed again after that, until Peter. Peter had stirred something in her, rekindling a thirst she thought she had quenched. Killing Sanderson was a well-plotted scheme, whereas the robber – wanna be book club supporter was a spur-of-the-moment act.

Sanderson, she'd investigated. She'd sat in wait at the Bookaneer that fateful night. She'd followed him to Grand Bend, stalked him, waited, watched the cameras, and made her move. He was drunk. He was frisky, and he was interested despite the ridiculous attire she wore. Sleeping with a homeless person satisfied some depraved bucket list for him.

Theresa had convinced Sanderson to take her home, securely hidden in his back seat. Once there, she gave him the Orphenadrine injection by jabbing it into his thigh while still in the car. The drug was her father's. The leather case which held the needle and a few shots of the drug was something she'd retained with the assorted knickknacks that reminded her of her parents. Sanderson had jumped at the prick and gotten out of the car, whispering, 'what was that?' worried his wife and child might hear him.

'A bee - Let's play a game,' she whispered back and pulled the noose from her bag. He was curious enough to let her place it over his head and confident enough not to fear her. Then his muscles went slack, and he sagged to his knees. Theresa quickly threw the rope over the naked joists in the garage's ceiling and pulled him to a standing position. He couldn't struggle. His head fell to the side, and his face turned purple.

She used all her strength to lift the dead weight and, with leverage from a workbench, managed to hoist him just an inch off his feet and tie the rope off on the bench's leg. Theresa listened as he gasped and placed the note in his sports jacket pocket. Just enough that it stuck out for someone to find. There, karma had been served. Sanderson had lynched Peter in the past and now hung from the rafters of his home.

She slipped out the garage's side door and navigated the yard when she was sure he was dead, avoiding cameras and motion lights. Of course, she had staked the house out and knew the motion lights over the side door didn't work. It was fated.

The armed robber, whose name she didn't know, was her next karmic example. After Peter's discovery in a session that his book club was being headed up by a man who had taken his head in revolutionary France, she couldn't just sit back and let him be taken advantage of.

Initially, she planned to join the group as invited and size the man up. The machete, her father's, sat next to her on the passenger seat alongside the dark, heavy costume she'd worn for all her karma killings. But as she sat in her car and saw that Peter wasn't letting him in, she felt a stab of pride. He was taking her advice. Then the fool Clare appeared, and the robbery commenced.

Theresa had decided then the man would die, and minutes later, he fled. She saw Peter come to the window. He was alive but scared. She turned her car around to follow the robber, watched him enter an underground apartment, and found herself in the alley behind his tired residence. She watched him diligently through the small window until he fell asleep, aided by a handful of pills.

Then, she dressed in her Karma Killer attire, slipping through the unlatched window, machete in hand, bashed him over the head with the blunt end, and tied him tightly to a chair.

She pulled his head back with a fist full of his hair when he regained consciousness and presented the note. His eyes widened as he read: *Karma has a Champion. They deserved it.* Signed: *The Karma Killer.* When he reached the *killer* portion of the note, all hope escaped his expression. He knew then that he was paying a karmic debt owed to him in this life and in the past - where he had all the power. He had taken Peter's head in the revolution, and she would pay that back in kind just as she had Sanderson.

She pushed his head down to reveal the back of his neck and raised her machete. One swing severed his spinal cord and was difficult to extract as he uttered a cry. Once freed, she swung again with incredible force to hack the head from its body. The weight of the severed head was much heavier than she'd expected and slipped from her grasp, hitting the tile with a wet thud, rolling on the floor as blood spit in heartbeats from the corpse's torso.

She picked the head up and placed it on the body's lap and the card atop the head. She waited for the heartbeats to cease so she could pass by without being hit by blood spurts.

The act didn't faze her. She knew exactly what she would do to the man. It merely needed to be played out. She didn't feel emotionally connected to the crimes. She was detached. It was as if she were watching the thing happen from a distance.

She drove home to wash up when she crawled back out the window. Peter would be safe from this man now. She only wished she'd completed the task before the robbery.

Clare was easy, she remembers. Taking her father's wheelchair, which he would use after prolonged stretches of gardening, she walked right into the gothic building and took the elevator up to the top floor. There are four penthouse suites in that posh building, and though Theresa had brought a prybar, she first tried Clare's door. It was unlocked, so she slowly pushed inward. Seeing Clare seated with her back to her, Theresa snuck up dressed in her Karma Killer outfit. Then Clare abruptly stood up, and Theresa cracked her on the back of the head with the steel prybar. The surprise of Clare's sudden movement forced a more devastating swing than Theresa had planned to throw. She thought she'd killed her then and there, but Clare groaned, lost consciousness, and fell onto the couch.

Theresa left her card on the coffee table and gently pushed over a potted plant and a vase to make it seem like there had been a struggle. Then she brought the wheelchair in and hefted Clare into it, placing a blanket over her lap and a ball cap on her head. Then they left, and when they made it to Theresa's car a few blocks away, she preceded to take Clare home.

Now what? Now the same detective who'd had the gall to question her on the beating deaths of her parent's murderers is sitting in his car, steaking out her home.

There could be only one explanation for it.

Chapter 35

Theresa is found out. She fucked up. The anxiety over the realization that she couldn't continue her good work in this life is a hit. They'd deserved their fates; of that, she had no question. Peter was a victim of their immoral acts reaching back hundreds of years. She'd sat listening to each of his tormented lives and conceived her plan to become The Karma Killer. It made sense and provided purpose to her work. They called her a serial killer. They called the murders unjust and despicable. They didn't know their past crimes. They didn't realize they would continue their assault on innocence in this life. They didn't understand the responsibility she had as a vigilante. They didn't know the pain and suffering she was preempting. The man responsible for her downfall couldn't solve her parent's case and arrest their murderers, but he's found her out.

Theresa moves through her house collecting things she would need while on the run. Throwing clothes and other items into her overnight bag, she lands on a photo of her parents. It stands in an ornate, silver frame on the buffet in the sitting room she had cleansed of the memory of their murders. But the new hardwood replacing the blood-soaked carpet was just window dressing on a darker stain that never really left her. She pauses at the photo and then picks it up, thrusting it into her bag. Damn him, she thinks. Damn him for spoiling everything. Nothing threaded the murders together save her calling card. Why did she feel inclined to announce each killing with a card? Was it to offset the guilt she felt over the murders? Was it to explain her reasoning? To ask forgiveness? No, she feels justified in the slayings. They were destined to play out their cruel intentions again. She was protecting Peter.

Was she a serial killer like they'd said in the newspapers and on television? The killings were all over the internet. Groups had surfaced trying to put the pieces together. Where was the motive? They looked like entirely unrelated events.

Now it would all be undone. Stupid girl, she chastises herself. Still, she's made it easier for Peter to live. Those deaths would free him up to live a full life. Regardless, she must run now. She must leave everything she's built upon her parents' untimely deaths and run.

A distant siren, and she feels her face flush with blood. Her heart pounds, and adrenaline releases anxieties thought long buried. The threat is real. The trial and victim statements. They wouldn't understand. They couldn't. She couldn't listen to them. She runs to the basement, where her father's gun sits in its lockbox. She opens it to reveal the revolver, then slips it into the bag with a dozen loose bullets. She couldn't be taken. She wouldn't.

She glances at Clare's still body slumped forward in the metal chair. *Is she dead?* Maybe. Her hand tightens around the grip of the pistol. She considers discharging the firearm into Clare's petite body, but 'karma' won't have been served if she kills her like that. Not really. Clare's heart must give out on her. It must be broken. Theresa places her fingers against Clare's windpipe. She's icy cold. There is a pulse, but it's irregular. She's close. It won't be long, little bird, Theresa thinks and moves up the stairs.

It's raining hard again, falling in sheets, as she peeks through the blinds in her living room. Satisfied she has what she needs, Theresa throws open the front door and dashes to her car. Once inside, she starts the engine to her father's '94 Pontiac and tears out of the driveway. Reflexively Theresa looks at the silhouette of Harlow. The rain is teeming down, and it's difficult to see three feet in front of her. The rain is an excellent cover. *Does he even know it's me?* The thought of 'where are you going?' gives her pause. The question of *where* hadn't entered her mind. The idea that she simply needed to run is all that is driving her after spotting the detective across the street. *He knew. How did he know? It doesn't matter how. That he's here is enough.*

Three cruisers pass her as she moves down her street: lights on but no sirens. She is cautious not to speed or forget her blinker when turning. They seem to have missed her. They continue to her house. She takes the corner and drives. She just drives.

They'll have notified everybody of her car's make, plate number, and color. The driving rain and darkness will suffice as camouflage for now, but what will happen when the storm retreats? She must formulate a plan. Will her bank account have been frozen? Where do people go to disappear? The woods? This option immediately becomes her plan. She knows a spot. Coldwater River Park in Kent County. It's where she planned to move Clare tomorrow. She can cover her car in the brush and decide where to go from there.

The anxiety has fully enveloped her now. She gulps in air, fighting off the sensations that follow a panic attack. Tears blur her vision, and she distractedly wipes them away with the sleeve of her jacket.

She'd done a good thing; she reminds herself. But Hell is often paved with good intentions, and she was convinced she was experiencing a Hell of sorts wrapped in this cocoon of anxious energy, fleeing from the law.

She wonders how she has gotten here. Her mind is ablaze with scenarios and analyses every choice she's made to arrive at this nightmare. But she never really had a choice. She couldn't save her parents, so she put that guilt into action with Peter. His enemies were her enemies. She'd done what the universe had demanded of her. What she knew she could not unknow, and she could not stand idly by and let a good man like Peter repeat a cycle that would stunt his evolutionary growth. Perhaps that is enough. Maybe she will be given another chance to continue her work in the next life? Perhaps her true purpose is yet to be announced.

Chapter 36

Harlow's gaze shifts from his phone to a car lacking daytime running lights as it passes him on the residential street in the torrential storm. He remembers his first car – a 1998 hatchback that didn't have daytime runners. *Who goes out in this? Oh, shit. Someone on the run!* He's been made. The reinforcements pull up next to him, three cruisers strong. He'd called them in to block off the street. He jumps out of his car and rushes to Theresa's house with two officers in tow. The grey car that was parked in the driveway is gone. He feels his face flush as his blood pressure soars. Had he just lost the Karma Killer?

With his jacket pulled over his head, shielding him from the downpour, he tries the front door – it's unlocked. "Search the house," he tells the officers.

Harlow calls into the station on Atwater St. to speak with tech services. They have Theresa's number, and so long as the phone is turned on, they can track her. This is welcome news. Harlow finds the basement door and descends the staircase.

BINGO. A slight female frame is bent over, forehead nearly touching her knees. She's secured to the chair, which sits in the middle of the unfinished basement. Harlow calls up the stairs for the officers to call an ambulance.

He studies the ropework and pulls it apart, careful not to let Clare fall forward and out of the chair. She smells of urine and sweat and weighs next to nothing. He carries her up the stairs and places her on a couch overlooking the storm as it rages outside. The lights in the house flicker once but remain on. Harlow checks Clare's pulse and opens her eyelids. Sleep has built up in the corners of her eyes, and her skin feels dry. She's dehydrated! The detective rushes into the kitchen and pours a glass of water. He finds a tea towel and wets it. When he returns to Clare's limp body, he slowly squeezes the towel over her mouth, allowing small water droplets to fall on her lips and tongue.

One of the officers returns with a clear garbage bag in hand; its contents look like the dark clothing worn by the Karma Killer. All the evidence Harlow needs is here. Now he needs to track Theresa and bring her back.

The ambulance arrives, and paramedics check Clare's vitals. They lift her onto the stretcher and wheel her out. "What hospital are you taking her to?" Harlow shouts after them. They reply, and Harlow calls Peter to inform him of Clare's status.

"It *was* Theresa," Peter feels betrayed. Harlow can hear it in his tone. "I'll go to the hospital right away. Thank you, Detective."

Harlow orders the officers to secure the scene and return his next call to the station. "Can you triangulate her position?"

"We're pinging her number and tracking her, Detective. I'm sending you the GPS location so you can follow. She's still moving."

Harlow receives the GPS tracker info on his phone and hurries out to his car. The rain is less heavy now. He could make up considerable time in the chase. "Don't involve Agent Garcia yet. Give me a half-hour head start. I don't want to spook her with FBI on the scene before I have a chance to bring her in."

"Understood, Detective. You have half an hour."

Harlow Starts his car and makes a U-turn in the wide, residential street. The GPS is running on his Mobile Data Computer now. He tears off in the direction Theresa had fled.

His thoughts are fluid. They jump from victim to victim and land on Clare. He hopes she will survive the ordeal. *What was Theresa's plan, death by starvation?* Clare was so slight he fears she might die. How did the girl he'd met 11 years earlier become this cold-blooded killer?

Harlow's phone rings. It's Peter. "Detective, I didn't explain myself when you told me about Sanderson. How I knew who your killer was."

Harlow lets Peter speak, "Please," he says.

"Sanderson appeared in one of my past life regression sessions with Theresa. He'd lynched me in that life. The man who robbed me, he'd also been a part of my past life. He'd beheaded me during the French revolution."

Harlow shakes his head at the explanation. Sanderson was hanged, and Zach was beheaded. "And what was Clare's crime? I assume you had a past with her as well."

"Yes," Peter says in a whisper; Harlow hears the telltale sound of bus doors opening. "She had broken my heart more than once."

"So, Clare's abduction somehow relates to that."

"I - I guess it must. I don't claim to understand why Theresa has done what she's done, but it sounds like she was protecting me in some twisted way."

"That's exactly what it sounds like," Harlow takes the on-ramp onto the highway. The rain is just a sprinkling now, but the sky is still dark.

"I can't help but feel partially responsible," Peter admits.

Harlow muffles a chuckle. "You're a good man, Peter. Don't lose any sleep over feeling responsible. Theresa is a big girl. She acted alone. You're as much a victim of these crimes as anyone. Just be glad you survived."

"Are Clare's chances good?"

"She was severely dehydrated," Harlow offers, not wanting to lead on that she has any better than a 50/50 chance. "No other clear signs of trauma."

"Thank you so much," Peter sighs. "I'm here now. I'll wait."

"I'm texting you Clare's mother's number. Would you please let her know where she is?"

"Absolutely. I'll call her right away."

"Goodbye, Peter. And good luck." Harlow hangs up and refocuses on Theresa's GPS coordinates. He's been on the road for two hours and making good time playing catch-up. He realizes Theresa has stopped moving but is still another fifteen minutes away. Harlow zooms in on the location. She's in a wooded area - a County Park with a working farm and trails through the dense wood along the Coldwater River.

Is she going to hoof it from there? In this weather? Or is she just taking the opportunity to hide out for a few hours until nightfall? He notices a river running north to south with a shiver of recognition, not far from her parked position.

As he approaches the entrance to the County Park, he wishes he could shut his lights off, but these new cars don't offer that option. The car creeps along the muddy, twisting drive. The forest comprises equal amounts of old-growth deciduous and evergreen trees. The trees and undergrowth are thick and lush. Rain returns but nothing like it was.

Harlow decides to stop his car and shut it off when the GPS tells him he's 50 yards from her position. The trek through the soft forest floor is trying on his bad knees. He sees the light of a phone move through the branches in the clearing and then disappear.

Chapter 37

Theresa had walked these woods a hundred times with her parents in her young life. Summers spent camping and standing up to her knees in the river to catch tadpoles, autumns identifying leaves, and winters cross-country skiing. Late morning conveys the sensation of dusk as the dreary clouds linger overhead, darkening the land, and the cool breeze settles into her bones. She pulls her bag of essentials from the passenger seat and activates the flashlight on her phone. The woods are deserted. The flashlight lands on a pair of eerie, shining eyes in the distance. *Raccoons, most likely.*

She shivers from the rain and pulls the hood over her head, wrapping her coat around her torso, imagining her father's hug. *It's not fair.* She shouldn't have to run like this. She shouldn't have to return to this place of youthful innocence as a fugitive.

She sees headlights dance through the line of trees as a vehicle winds its way through the trail from the road to the parking lot. Her heart races over the thought, and sweat mingles with rain on her palms. *They've come for me. How did they know?* She turns the flashlight app off and realizes her mistake. *My phone. They've tracked my phone.* A stupid misstep, but she's hardly a hardened criminal with the wherewithal to plan something like this. She turns her phone off just the same. The car may just be a couple of teenagers out for an evening make-out session. She remembers those days too. They seem a lifetime ago now. The headlights fall on her, and she steps behind her car, now covered in branches and other forest camouflage. The vehicle stops a few yards away, and a door opens.

"Theresa," a voice calls out. *It's him. It's Harlow.* Her heart sinks, and anxiety enters. She takes another step back and turns to review her escape route. The light of a full moon provides a momentary glimpse of the forest floor, returning a second later behind the fast-moving, charcoal clouds.

"I'm not coming with you," she returns to Harlow's silhouette. *Is it moving closer?* Adrenaline floods her muscles, and she feels the warmth build in her thighs, bending her knees, forcing her into a sprinting position. Her trembling hand falls to the pistol secured in her pant pocket. It's heavy and a reminder of her present predicament. She doesn't want to draw it, but destiny waits for no one. The progression therapy she'd done on herself tells her that much. There's no reason to wait and find out if the detective will charge.

Chapter 38

Harlow sees Theresa plain as day. Like a deer caught in the headlights, he thinks. She's terrified. Her fixed expression in the momentary moonlight gives that much away, but her stance, muscles taught, and frame slightly bent over, ready to flee, articulate there will be a chase.

"Let's get out of the rain and talk," he pleads, hoping to ease her apparent angst. "I need your help, Theresa." She steps back, and Harlow takes a tentative step forward. *She's going to run goddamn it.* He's never done well with the chase, and he doesn't like his odds in these dark, slippery woods. He could call in back up and have a 'copter here within the hour, but that isn't how he wants this to progress. He's mindful not to place his hand on his weapon. He doesn't want her to run. He wants to earn her trust. The trust he'd lost during her parent's investigation; when he'd questioned Theresa on her whereabouts the night the junkies were murdered. He knew he had lost her as an ally that day. She had provided a reasonable alibi. He didn't like asking but explained he had done so to eliminate her as a suspect. Still, her eyes were so full of hate over the accusation that he felt like an asshole – his self-loathing over the way the case had ended solidified his decision to drop it.

Now he stands just a few yards away from the girl who has become a serial killer. There is no question now. Had he somehow created her from his failure as a detective? Had he caught the meth heads before they'd been murdered, maybe she wouldn't have become this vigilante killer? The notes gave the reasons she killed, as weak as they were: *They deserved it.* No one can predict the future. This he believes adamantly. Past lives or not, there is no way to know they would reenact a past life vendetta. Theresa was wrong to have done what she'd done. She would have to answer for her crimes. If he, in any way, played a part in her becoming the woman she is today, then he too should answer for his ineptitude.

"Please come out of the rain, Theresa. I only want to talk." Saying the words aloud, he realizes he isn't very convincing. *Goddamn it. Fuck it.* He takes two more steps forward. Her body cringes, and he watches her head dart to her right. He hears the river rushing over rock just beyond a grouping of brush and allows himself a quick look. *What's her plan? To sprint off and cross the river?* The rains have created a problematic current. The water appears to be waist-high at its deepest. He is determined to stop her before she makes a break for it, but how? Could he fire his gun at her? Could he hit her leg in this misty rain, just wounding her? Would his aim be true? Unlikely. He might kill her. He might miss altogether. He couldn't outrun her. Not with her clear lead and his aversion to the chase.

"Please," he says, his tone less confident than he'd like. Then she bolts. *Goddamn it.* Harlow bounds forward, and the chase is on. Once Theresa is outside the reach of his sightlines, darkness envelops her. He follows in the general direction she's moving but can only guess at her trajectory. He hears splashing on the river's edge and knows her plan. A quick twist to his right and his knee fails him. He drops, grasping the injured appendage, muffling a cry.

He staggers to his feet and tests the knee. It's not good. He could be out of the chase. Still, he manages to make the river and calls out to her again, this time with his gun drawn. She's made it to the opposite edge and turns to face him.

Chapter 39

"You were right to question me on the deaths of those two junkies, Detective," Theresa shouts across the creek, challenging the thunder. "I know why they killed my parents. So, *I* killed them. I saw the same scenario play out two hundred years ago."

Harlow keeps his pistol trained on the suspect despite the wind picking up and the driving rain. *Two hundred years ago. What is she on about?* "Stay where you are, Theresa. Just stay where you are," he calls back, concerned that he will have to follow on his weakened knee if she flees into the woods.

"It's a pattern," Theresa yells. "People hurt each other over and over across many lives. Those meth heads killed my parents because of what I'd done to them in 1814. I'd killed their parents, Harlow. *Me.* It's my fault my parents died at their hands. It was my cross to carry, not yours! I had to end the cycle." She wipes the wet, long dark hair from her forehead. The distance between them is just a few yards, but the uneven, rocky path through the river seems impossible with a damaged knee. Harlow watches Theresa as the winds bend the long grass surrounding her. She looks almost ghostly. Her body relaxes, no longer threatening to run. "The others, they hurt my client. They would do it again."

"You can't know that," Harlow calls back, favoring his bad knee. "Come back with me, Theresa. You can tell your story there."

"They died in the manner they killed Peter," her voice is waning. "They deserved nothing less."

He's losing her, and he's losing his patience. "They didn't deserve *that* – what you did to them. They didn't." He shakes his head and wipes his face. "If you come back with me and confess, your sentence will be reduced. You'll receive a full psych evaluation. Running isn't the answer."

"It's a pattern woven into the fabric of time, Detective." She's ignoring him. "It's karma!" There it is - the full confession from The Karma Killer. She raises her hand, revealing a pistol. It happens in a flash. Harlow swears he witnesses a burst of lightning ignite the darkness, but then Theresa falls back into the tall grass lining the river's edge.

Harlow's index finger remains hard against the trigger. He barely felt the gun kick and realized he'd fired on his suspect. He has only discharged his firearm at someone once before. The sensation is unwanted. He grimaces and holsters his weapon. Harlow begins the arduous journey across the rising river, his wounded knee carefully navigating the loose stones not to experience another shock of pain. The water is cold, and he finds comfort in this as his injured knee cools at the deepest level.

Theresa relives the end she feared would come. The bullet punched through her flesh, facia, and muscle, splintering bone to push through soft organs. The pain is indescribable. The end - indisputable. She tastes blood on her tongue. It's thick and doesn't retreat down her throat. It rises into her mouth and spills down her chin. This is serious, Theresa concludes. *This is it.* She falls backward, her legs suddenly weak, unable to carry her. Laying on the cold, wet ground, she's reminded of a life she'd relived through regression, dying from a devastating musket wound during the War of 1812. It was the same life where she'd killed a couple defending their land. It seems that end has been revisited on her in this life. She almost laughs ironically at the thought, but the pain in her chest stymies the instinct. She takes comfort in her belief that she will be born again. She takes solace in knowing.

Reaching the far side, Harlow finds Theresa squirming in agony from the bite of the bullet. His flashlight lands on her where blood spits up out of her mouth and sprays her face. The rain does its best to wash it away, but she coughs it up again and again. Her glasses have flown from her face. Harlow bends down to assess the damage. He pulls at her buttoned blouse and finds the hole. Then he takes her hand and places it over the wound.

"Press down on it," he tells her. Theresa screams out in pain as she obeys. Harlow finds his phone and calls 911.

"I - I think I saw the future," Theresa manages. Harlow leans in to shelter her from the rain. "I'd wronged you in a ... past life, Detective ..."

Harlow feels compelled to hear her out. This would be her dying declaration, he knows. Help is too far removed from this remote park in Kent County – the city of Grand Rapids is too far to save her. She is losing blood at a rapid pace. He hangs up on the operator. "What do you mean?"

"I - hurt you in the past." Speaking becomes difficult for her. Breathing is labored. "You've repaid a Karmic debt tonight ..." Theresa's eyelids flicker. "It was destined to end like this for me," she coughs and cringes, "at your hands."

"You've *never* hurt me, Theresa. I know I failed you, but you've never hurt *me*." Harlow had always regretted that her parent's murderers had turned up dead before he'd had the opportunity to affect justice on them. That Theresa has admitted to killing them tonight makes him nauseous. If he'd caught them first... maybe she wouldn't have become the person she has.

Theresa's free hand reaches for the detective's face and lightly touches his unshaven chin. "It's not your fault," she begins in a defeated and slight tone as if reading his thoughts, "destiny waits for no one... and no one escapes their destiny." She coughs violently, spittle landing on Harlow's drenched shirt. "Tell Peter I did it... for him." Her hand falls to her side, her arm landing in an unnatural position, her head tilts to the left, eyes open.

Harlow checks her pulse and reluctantly closes her eyes. She's gone. He gathers up Theresa's gun and, as is routine, opens the cylinder. *Empty.* She'd contrived the whole thing. He falls back to a seated position on the wet earth. *Death by cop.* But it was more than that. She'd felt destiny's pull and allowed him to fire on her. Killing her. She knew this would be her end. Perhaps she was telling the truth. Her truth. That in reliving the past, you see the future. Maybe past lives were real. Perhaps they offered some sense of closure on the present. Some deeper dialogue. Maybe. For the present, Harlow hears the approach of several vehicles through the woods. The FBI agent will be among them. Harlow will have some explaining to do, but even with The Karma Killer dead, the trail of evidence leading him to this end is overwhelming.

He remains seated next to Theresa's body, his knee aching. Steam escapes her as the rain tapers off. His focus defaults to the rush of the river behind him. Something is calming about it. Something reassuring. He lets it carry the weight of the event away, stands unsteadily, and waves the officers over.

Chapter 40

Captain Anderson looks stunning in full dress uniform at the podium outside city hall. She addresses the media concerning the end of their city's recent reign of terror.

"The person called The Karma Killer has been apprehended," she says, holding her head high and nodding to Detective Harlow in his full-dress uniform, currently experiencing a mix of emotions over the way the case played out. He's nervous over the announcement and regrets having shot and killed Theresa. It's never the way a cop wants a case to go, but at least it's closure. Detroit will be safer, and the people will feel the killing is justified.

"The lead detective, William Harlow, had a difficult task in bringing the serial killer to justice, but justice has been served." She motions for him to approach the podium and opens a small box containing a medal. "For your unquestionable service to Detroit and those you've sworn to protect, I am honored to present the Meritorious Service medal."

Harlow nods at his captain, acknowledging the important honor and Anderson pins the medal to his dress uniform. Harlow experiences a warmth in his chest, competing amidst the cold that has descended upon him over the shooting. He's proud of his investigative work but ashamed of its conclusion. Still, he has Theresa's dying words to hold onto. He had no choice over the outcome. He was merely playing a part.

Anderson shakes his hand, as do the Mayor of Detroit and Chief of Police. Anderson returns her attention to the gathering crowd. "You can feel safe again in your city knowing men like Detective Harlow have dedicated their careers to that end."

Applause rips through the crowd, and Anderson takes questions from her favorite media personalities. Harlow remains by her side to field any queries the captain decides to pass on to him. He removes his peaked cap and tucks it under his right arm, staring out at those who have come to offer their respect for his service. It's one of the warmer days in June with a clear sky above. He welcomes a slight breeze as it caresses his face.

Can she forgive me? It is a question he'll never have an answer for, but one he's felt moved to ask himself time and again. Harlow fights back tears as his eyes begin to water.

It's only the breeze, he tells himself.

When the event concludes, he returns to the station on Atwater St., where he and Anderson share a drink in her office. It's his favorite. 18-year-old scotch from an obscure distillery in the Scottish Highlands. They clink their glasses and sit to enjoy the spirit.

"I hope you're happy with your success, Will," she tells him, sizing him up with those intelligent eyes. "I know we don't like to end a case like that, but you reacted as any of us would have. Remember that."

Anderson's argument helps Harlow relax into the leather chair. "What's your take on past lives, Jill?" He uses her given name as is customary in these situations.

Anderson shrugs and turns her glass, wiping the bottom with a tissue. "I live in the real world – in the here and now. I can't be chasing ghosts."

"But that's what I've been doing," Harlow says, placing his glass on her desk. "Chasing ghosts. It was a near-impossible case."

"And you solved it," she smiles at him. "You're a great detective, Will. All your successes speak to that, but this one," she drinks from the short glass.

"Maybe so," he doesn't enjoy being complimented for his work, and today's spectacle was proof of that. "I'd have liked to have had a longer conversation with the woman. You know my history with her now."

Anderson leans in, her expression severe. "You didn't *create* her," she explains. "Get that through your head. You're not that important." She winks at him, and he barks out a laugh. "We all make choices. She made hers and died for it. You did your best on her parent's case. She took it upon herself to find and murder the men responsible. That's on her. None of it is on you."

Harlow nods, smiling. He respects his captain, and she makes a lot of sense. Still, this is his burden to bear.

"Thank you for the drink, Jill; there's someone I need to see."

Jill nods and pushes the bottle toward him as he stands. "I don't really like this shit," she admits. "Take it with you, would you?" Harlow accepts the gift and heads to his car.

At the hospital, Harlow meets Clare, sitting up in her bed, an IV delivering hydration and nourishment with Peter and an older woman at her bedside. Clare's already slight frame looks emaciated. Sunken cheeks and her clavicle protruding from under her hospital gown. Peter stands abruptly and shakes his hand enthusiastically.

"We're so grateful, Detective," he tells him. "Uh, this is Clare's mother, Mrs. Hastings. Uh, Jane Hastings." Peter waves a hand at the older woman. She's an attractive fifty-something with a tight braid and a stern, pale but made-up face. She stands next to take his hand.

"Ma'am," Harlow greets her with a handshake and then looks to Clare. "I just wanted to make sure they're treating you well."

"Thank you, Detective," Clare says with a nod, her voice still weak and hollow from the ordeal. She raises a slender arm to shake his hand. Harlow feels compelled to offer his. She is cool to the touch, but he surmises she's on the mend.

"I only wish I could have found you sooner," he smiles awkwardly and steps back. "Peter was integral in my investigation," he submits. "We came to the same conclusion together. The evidence pointed to one person."

"Oh?" Clare says in a whisper, looking Peter's way, "you haven't told me everything."

Mrs. Hastings, the mother, looks from Harlow to Peter and smiles brightly at him. Winning points with the future mother-in-law, Harlow thinks, comically. Good, he deserves it.

"Well, it looks like you're all settled. I'll let you three get back to it. I'm happy to know you're well." Harlow nods at Clare, and she at him. Peter walks him out of the room and stops a moment in the busy hallway.

"You didn't have to say that in there," Peter says modestly.

"I figured you for the type who wouldn't have said it yourself, so," Harlow places a hand on Peter's shoulder. "One good turn deserves another. Besides, I just made you a hero to the mother," he winks, and Peter almost blushes.

"Don't skip any more of your meetings," Harlow warns him. "You'll need them more than ever after this. PTSD isn't something you can run from."

Peter nods and grunts his agreement, "I'll be going back, and I'll be attending therapy with Clare as well. It's a kind of couple's therapy."

Harlow almost leaves it at that, but a nagging question surfaces. "Did Theresa help you? I don't mean by murdering your boss and the thief. Did she help you with the regression therapy?"

Peter leans against the hallway wall, thoughtfully, as if calculating his answer. "The journey was interesting, and I gained an understanding of my shortcomings, so yes, in a way, it helped. I have work to do, but identifying other triggers that lay under the skin, so to speak, offered clarity."

"Good, I'm glad she helped. She made some radical choices I can't support, no one could, but that was her journey, I suppose." Harlow decides not to impart Theresa's final words directed to Peter. *Tell him I did it for him.* It feels like this would hinder his healing rather than assist in it.

Peter nods, pushing away from the wall. He offers his hand to Harlow again, and they shake. Nothing more is said.

Harlow feels a little lighter, knowing Theresa wasn't all bad. If his failure as a detective set her on a course where she could help people in one capacity, that would have to be enough.

Whether he would consider past lives as truth or not, he's come away with a new respect for karma. He opens the door to his matte black Dodge Charger in the parking lot and reaches into his pocket, pulling out his lighter. It's been a constant in his life since Tiff left him. It supplied pain where he thought he'd lost it. He used to think it made him stronger. Now he considers it a silly obsession and tosses the lighter as far as he can throw it.

"That's a hundred dollar fine, asshole," he tells himself, sitting hard into the driver's seat. He slams his door and drives back to Atwater St. station, where a recent murder demands his attention. *When will people learn?*

Chapter 41

The outpouring of affection in the form of Get-Well cards, texts, emails, posts on social media, and even letters from strangers has been an uplifting experience for Clare. She'd accepted two radio interviews and one local morning television show to tell her story. Free advertising is most welcome as an executive to a budding social responsibility platform, and she's not above mentioning it. Still, the haunting memories of her time in that basement have caused occasional panic attacks. But Peter has been a phenomenal support to her and says passing his knowledge on has helped him leaps and bounds in his own recovery.

She can't imagine loving someone more than she loves Peter. Their relationship has blossomed over the past few weeks, and love has followed. She has wanted to show him her gratitude in a unique way. Today the news came in the form of a business contract from overseas.

The two sit at 'Quoth the Raven' for a meal described in Poe's haunting narrative. It's delicious, and when the plates are cleared, Clare orders them a cognac each.

"I don't really like this stuff, you know," Peter says, looking mockingly debonaire, swirling the short brandy snifter in one hand.

"I don't care; it's tradition now," she replies giddily, sipping at the amber liquid. "How about that guy," she discreetly points out a man wearing black leather slacks and a button-up, mostly unbuttoned, revealing manscaped chest hair.

"Ah, that's an easy one, Jim Morrison," Peter tells her. "Maybe he can be persuaded to sing us a song." He laughs at himself and chooses from the bar's growing gathering of young professionals. "The lady with the flashy purse. Who was she?"

Clare loves that they've settled on this game when out. It's uniquely theirs. "Hmm, she could be Zsa Zsa Gabor. No, wait, what's his name? Karl Lagerfeld. She has a masculine aura."

Peter laughs harder than he means to, stifling a snort over the fact she'd picked a man for *Flashy Purse.* "I like that; I was a woman once in my past."

"You told me that," Clare reminds him, "I like your feminine side."

Peter snorts at this, setting his glass down. "How about the big guy in the sports jacket?"

"Andre the Giant," Clare submits. "His hands are huge!"

"I like him with Jim," Peter studies the two, just feet apart, emersed in the commotion at the bar.

"Maybe," Clare looks thoughtfully from one man to the other. "Do you think Andre might hurt Jim?"

"Jim's a lean but sturdy fella," Peter supplies, "I feel like the two could find a position that satisfies both." He says this pragmatically, and Clare giggles over the visual.

"Shall we work our magic?"

"I hate being wrong about these things. What do you want to put on it?"

"It's about the journey, not whether we win or lose."

"I'll put breakfast in bed on the table." Peter offers. "For one weekend."

"Those are high stakes," Clare ponders the proposition. "You're on."

After the restaurant, they return to Clare's penthouse suite. Sharing Clare's bed, Peter feels the flush of love in her embrace and his. Detroit lay before them 33 floors below. Her floor-to-ceiling windows capture the essence of the city. Clare is the vice-president of a multinational media company overseeing environmental solutions the world over, and she heads up their social media department. She is a diamond in the rough. She is what the world needs right now and what Peter possesses. He's reminded of their first date and how he'd told her that he expected her to pay for dinner. Now, staring at the fine finishes to the room and the painting beside the ensuite, he realizes why she hadn't scoffed at that.

They make love, their hips locking together, fingers tangled in each other's hair, pulling, caressing, exploring. Clare rolls over, glistening with sweat on her taught, small frame. She'd recovered nicely from the malnutrition and dehydration at the hands of Theresa in short order.

"About that bookstore," she says, sitting up on the bed, legs crossed, fluffing the pillows. "I don't want to lose it."

"I still have my job," Peter says, sitting up to meet her. "We won't lose it. I'm in touch with the second ex-Mrs. Sanderson. She's very happy to keep me on."

"I spoke to her too," a sparkle enters Clare's eyes. "She is quite a lovely woman and very agreeable."

Peter is captivated. "Agreeable in what way?"

"I know how much you love The Bookaneer, Peter. I want it to be yours." She turns to retrieve something from the marble bedside table. It's a file folder. She hands it to him. "And now it is." She's beaming.

Peter can't believe his eyes. The papers support what Clare is telling him. She's bought The Bookaneer, and it's in *his* name! He looks up at her, mouth agape, unable to express his gratitude. "I – Clare, I," Clare's long thin finger pressed against his lips.

"I got it for a steal," she follows this statement with her customary nod. "I love you, Peter."

Peter's heart soars. He thought he knew this but hearing it for the first time is bliss. He doesn't fight the tears as they roll down his face. Placing the document at his side, he folds himself into Clare, enveloping her naked body. He feels her heartbeat against him. Their sweat mingles, and they become electric. The warmth of the moment is transcendental.

"I love you, Clare."

"I know," she replies confidently, nods, and they fall into each other again, locked in a mutual embrace of love and understanding.

An Excerpt from Her Past's Present

AMAZON REVIEWS

"In telling Tess's story, author Michael Poeltl hints that there may be a method to the madness that constitutes daily life." – Rose Keefe

"Very well written. I can't wait to read what he comes up with next!" – R.F.

"This book captured my attention almost immediately. I couldn't put it down. Loved the story. It still has me thinking about it." – P. Miller

"Each page of the book brings you closer to Tess and what her purpose in life is. This author leads you ever so slowly and subtly deeper into the well-plotted story." = kissablysweet1

"Highly recommended!" – E. Joyce Caudle

"This is a terrific novel! It is very well written and moves right along with a gripping storyline and several plot twists." - Norma

GOODREADS REVIEWS

"I gave this one 5 cheers out of 5 because it really asks some hard questions." – Melanie Adkins

"I was drawn into the characters and the story right away." - Lynn

With mysteries and past lives to unravel, you're sure to enjoy **Her Past's Present.** *Unable to cope with a deteriorating existence and encroaching anxiety, Tess checks herself into a mental health facility. Inside, she meets Tebor, another patient who claims to know her* *from a previous life. Hopeful she can heal her present by making peace with her forgotten past, Tess becomes receptive to the idea of past-life regression. She is assisted in her journey by Madhiva, a nurse skilled in hypnosis and past-life regression, and her psychiatrist, Dr. Samuelson, who uncovers a family secret that may send Tess to a dark place where no healing force can reach her.*

A sample has been provided below with a link to buy. Thank you for reading Killing Karma. I hope you find Her Past's Present just as enticing.

Available in paperback and ebook

Chapter One
September 15th, 2:00 am

It wasn't your fault. These are healing words, something Tess's therapist had her write out a thousand times when she was twelve. It became her mantra, a reassurance that what had happened to her baby brother could in no way be her fault.

Today, fifteen years after the suicide that had devastated her life and her parents' lives, she finds power in those words once more.

"I'm sorry," says Sam, her husband, standing stock-still in front of her. All that separates them is the granite-topped island situated in the middle of a kitchen under renovation. It is the only working surface available to lean on should he confirm her fears.

"Please," she pleads. "Please just tell me it doesn't mean anything. Tell me it was just the one time, and I can forgive you." She isn't hopeful for this outcome but can't bear the thought of the consequences that follow such an act. To be a single mother amidst all the renovations and bills and contractors and sleepless nights has overwhelmed her the past few days. Her already pale complexion is rapidly fading to a sickly, almost translucent white.

His head drops slowly, his eyes studying the grout lines framing the new tile at his feet. His heart isn't in this. He was far from ready to tell his wife of five years he'd met someone else; that since the last month of her pregnancy, he'd been seeing another woman. Sam's decided that that is a significant amount of time, and he is very much committed to this new woman. But not at all ready to tell his wife.

"Tess." He struggles with her name. His chin begins to tremble.

"Please, tell me it will be okay." She begs. "Tell me that you love me."

"I *do* love you, goddamn it," he manages through clenched teeth. His fist falls with a weak thump on the black granite counter while his other hand finds his face, defending her from his diminishing façade. He jerks and cries into his shield, turning away from Tess.

"Then why?" Tess begs, slowly sinking to her knees, coming to rest on the dusty tile, her back landing against the cupboard of the island.

"I don't know why." He turns and slides down the opposite side of the island. "I don't know."

"Please don't leave me with nothing," she begs.

"If I had an answer, I'd give it."

"*Please.*"

"I don't have an answer for you. I haven't an answer for *myself.*"

Her voice cracks. "If you love me, be with me."

"Don't you think I want that? Don't you think I *want* to be happy here?"

"You're not happy?"

"You know I'm not."

"I'm sorry if I haven't had the time to put into you. We have a baby."

"Jesus, I know we have a baby, and I love her, but I feel like the walls are closing in on me."

Tess shifts uncomfortably, the thin fabric of her pajama pants offering little insulation from the cool tile. "It's okay to feel trapped, but you need to talk to me."

"It's not *you.*"

"Then what?"

"*Me.* It's me."
It's not your fault. She tells herself. *It's not your fault.*

Chapter Two
October 15th, Monday

Tess is up with her daughter. It's 3:30 in the morning. This is the second time tonight, and she only put Emilia down at ten. At six months old, Tess had hoped Emma would have gotten into a pattern of sleep that would take her through the night. Even if she wasn't going to bed until later in the evening, at least sleeping through the night would be a blessing. But neither was happening, and now that she no longer has Sam to lean on, her days and nights seem to run together.

Sitting in Emilia's room, rocking gently to the soothing sounds of her daughter feeding at the bottle, Tess wonders, as she does every night at this time, *what next?* It has been a month since Sam left and nearly that long since she'd heard from him. He left her with everything, including the bank account. She knows she could complete the renovations on their apartment and live comfortably for the remainder of the year if it came to that, but she misses him endlessly; his presence in her bed, his turn with Emilia overnight, dinners, anticipating his return from work, adult conversation.

Tess cries silently over the baby, now convulsing to repress this reaction to her life. Every feeding ends up like this now; Tess crying over her infant daughter, a myriad of what if's tormenting her. *It wasn't your fault;* she reminds herself. *There is nothing you could have done to change the outcome.* Emilia, now sleeping, Tess lays her in the crib and, careful not to make a noise, sneaks out of her room.

It's now that the exhaustion of the day, both physical and emotional, hits her. With the last feeding of the night over, the long stretch of wakefulness begins until morning. Tess has not been able to sleep past four in the morning since Sam left, and with the relentless barrage of scenarios attacking her at her most vulnerable, there is no point in trying. Even lying in bed is a challenge, reading a book is a lost cause, and nothing silences the onslaught of questions. So, like every morning before sunrise, Tess drags her weakened spirit across the bedroom and into the nearly finished kitchen to begin her day.

After she makes a pot of coffee, she sits in front of a pile of bills she has had no time or inclination to pay. This spurs another panic attack. The first had happened the night after Sam had left. The experience was frightening, to say the least, and this was no different. It comes on without warning, starts in her left hand, then travels up her arm and attacks her shoulder. The feeling resembles so closely a description Tess had read on heart attacks that she immediately moves her right hand to her chest. Sure enough, the pain enters her chest, and Tess grips her left breast, willing the pain away.

Nothing can make you feel more confident that you're having a heart attack than a substantial panic attack. Even a heart attack either takes you within seconds or goes mostly unnoticed. A panic attack - on the other hand - goes on and on, and with each passing minute, your heart fills with dread that: *this time, it really is a heart attack!*

Tess fumbles with her tablet and punches in a search for panic attack symptoms. This technique settled her nerves enough to allow the attack to subside three days earlier. Finding the page once more, she scrolls down, reading hungrily in anticipation of the pins and needles sensation in her arms dissipating. Breathing in and out slowly also assists in alleviating the building panic. Each breath is an exercise in concentration.

After ten minutes, the symptoms leave as suddenly as they'd appeared. Feeling one hundred years older now, Tess sits; bent over the dining room table, head in folded arms. Then the baby cries.

It seems that she will be given no quarter today, and with the men coming to complete the kitchen in just a few short hours, Tess predicts a difficult day of electric drills and skill saws buzzing in her ear, while she and Emilia shut themselves into her bedroom to watch cartoons.

* * * * *

As nine o'clock approaches, the buzzer sounds, and Tess lets the men in with all their noisy equipment. She's happy to know the work will end after today, or so she's been told, but the barrage of questions concerning the specifics of the job is more than she can handle. This is their sixth time in the apartment, and Tess is well versed in how to make small talk. She points out the coffee maker with a full pot brewing on the counter and relays her plans with the baby for the day.

The foreman assures Tess they will be done today and out of her hair for good, barring any unforeseen difficulties. She nods and realizes she's been staring at the man. He looks inquisitively at her and asks whether there is something else. Tess, embarrassed, shakes her head.

"Sorry. Just tired is all."

"If I have any questions for you, I'll come knock on your door." He smiles and turns to accept a coffee from his apprentice.

Tess turns around and walks quickly to her room with Emma on her hip. It has been a long time since she's even considered the company of a man other than her husband but fixed in that gaze, she felt a sudden yearning for the unshaven foreman dressed in a white tee, beige overalls, and steel-toed boots.

In her bedroom, Tess catches herself in the vanity mirror and stops. Studying her reflection, she chastises herself.

"Look at you; nobody would want *you.*" Her hair is in knots, and her face is blotchy from the embarrassment she felt breaking eye contact with the foreman. She had done nothing to fix her appearance since waking up in preparation for their arrival, she hadn't even considered it. How could she have let herself go like this; she wonders. Glancing over at the collage of wedding photos still adorning her wall, she sets the baby down on her bed and pulls them down, tossing them into the corner. The glass shatters on one of the frames, and she again curses herself. She had thought leaving them in place served one of two purposes: Either Sam would return, and everything would be as it was, or she was steeling herself against him. Nothing had changed, though. Not in the month since he had disappeared. He hadn't returned to them, nor had she felt stoic against the black and white memories. She decides that she lives in a Mausoleum, a sad memorial to a marriage that didn't work.

* * * * *

That afternoon the work is completed as promised, and as the apprentice cleans up, the foreman knocks on Tess's door.

"All done," he says. Tess opens the door and smiles at him. She's made herself up, put on something more appropriate than the tights and loose sweater she'd been wearing to greet them, and walked to the kitchen with Emilia again resting on her hip.

"Wow, that looks really nice," she tells them. "I couldn't imagine it finished for the longest time."

As the men clear out of the apartment, tools in tow, the foreman hangs back a moment to collect his check. Tess places Emma on the floor in front of the TV and writes out the remainder of what's owed him on the island counter. She pauses, wondering whether she could ask him out for a drink sometime. She feels she needs to recover from the verbal beating she gave herself earlier in the day. A date would do that.

"Say, Remy, right?" She keeps her eyes on the check while she addresses him.

"Yes. Tess, right?"

"Yes, um, I wondered if you wanted to, I mean, maybe you'd like to get a drink sometime?" Tess feels her face flush. Her gaze remains on the counter.

"Oh, uh, I can't, but I would like to." He pulls a ring from his pocket and places it back on his finger. "I, uh, I take it off when I'm working."

Tess glances over and sees that his ring finger now wears a gold band. She stands up straight and hands his check to him, red-faced. "I'm so sorry. I mean, for me, not that you're married. I loved being married." She smiles awkwardly and walks to the door. "Listen, I'll, um, give you good references if you need them. Great work. Thanks again." She can't stop talking now, wishing the moment away.

"Hey, I'm honored, seriously." He tells her from the hall, quickly studying her own decorated ring finger.

"Oh, you don't have to say that. I'm okay, I understand." She runs a hand up and down the baby's back nervously.

"Well, you take care and enjoy your new kitchen." He bows out and heads towards the elevator, where his apprentice is waiting. Tess closes the door and sinks to the floor, humiliated.

Chapter Three
Tuesday, 3:00 am

Tess wakes with a start. Her heart is pounding, and she feels a chill on her back as she sits up. She's soaked through her nightshirt, and her hair is matted to one side of her face. She peels her shirt off and ties her hair back, lifting it off her neck. Looking at the alarm clock, she sees it's nearly time for Emilia to wake for her feeding. It's not particularly hot in the house; in fact, it's quite cool, *so why all the sweat?* Bad dreams, she faintly recalls.

Tess moves to the other side of the bed, avoiding the large damp circle, and lies down again. *Pathetic*, she thinks; that she still practices sleeping on her side of the bed while *his* remains vacant. Then the dream which woke her reveals itself in sporadic scenes; flashes of memory dance behind her eyelids.

There was a war going on outside her home. Not her current home, but her home all the same. It was dark save one electric light flickering with each vibration. Plaster fell on her each time a sound more threatening than thunder exploded overhead. The last thing she remembers of the dream was searching helplessly through the rubble of her home for her children, crying out to them, panic-stricken, wishing her husband was there.

I can't even escape into my dreams anymore, she tells herself, placing both hands over her face. The idea that she may find no peace in sleep now devastates her. She surrenders to the anxiety and turns to sob into the pillow, a pillow that still carries Sam's scent.

On this night, Emilia does not wake for her 4 am feeding, and Tess manages to collapse back into sleep after an exhausting hour of crying. At 7 am, she rolls over to look at the time. The house is silent. Tess is suddenly overcome by fear. *How could Emilia not be awake if she hadn't eaten in the night?* She hurries out of bed and rounds the hallway to her daughter's bedroom. She rushes in and finds Emilia on her stomach, in her crib. She is still. Tess is afraid to touch her. She's afraid to know. She's heard of crib death in infants; she's heard of all kinds of awful ways a child might die.

Emilia coughs, and Tess's heart leaps. She reaches down and pulls Emilia up to her chest. The baby is blurry-eyed and begins to cry. Tess savors the moment, hugging her and tearing up.

"Oh, Emma," she says over and over. "I love you; I love you; I love you."

Emilia settles down, and Tess walks her to the kitchen, opens the fridge, and retrieves a bottle of formula. She had tried to breastfeed early on, but after a month of aggressive pumping, she became discouraged and decided to go with formula. This did nothing to encourage her that she was a good mother, and she berated herself each time thereafter, she prepared a bottle of store-bought baby formula.

Once the bottle is warmed, Tess sits on the couch and thumbs at the television converter for a children's show. Emilia is happily feeding on the bottle when the phone rings.

"Hello," she answers, more enthusiastically than she'd meant to.

The other end is silent, so she repeats herself, this time with a hint of irritation in her voice.

Still nothing from the caller. Tess listens attentively, furrowing her brow as she leans into the earpiece. The caller hasn't hung up. They haven't done *anything*. Emilia lets out a satisfied burp and goes back to feeding.

"Sam?" She waits for some response. "Sam, is that you?" The phone drops at the other end. Tess jerks back from the receiver and hangs up. She looks down at her daughter.

"Your Daddy says hi." She smiles painfully and brushes her thin fingers through Emilia's short blonde hair.

The phone rings again, and this time Tess checks the call display. *Unknown number.* Well, maybe it was, and maybe it wasn't. She would take some comfort in believing it was Sam and let it ring.

Chapter Four
Tuesday, 1:00 pm

Tess keeps a lunch date with a friend from her office that afternoon. Amanda asked Tess more than once to bring Emilia in so everyone could ogle over her, but Tess found one reason after another as to why she couldn't. Now, a month into her separation, she couldn't imagine facing the humiliation of an explanation.

Seated outside a trendy café, Emma resting comfortably in her stroller beside her; she waits for Amanda to arrive. Tess waves as she watches her friend approach from across the street. She stands to meet her, and the women hug.

"You look fan-*fucking*-tastic!" she tells Tess.

Embarrassed by the compliment, Tess waves it off, shaking her head as she sits.

"Shut up," Amanda continues. "I have to starve myself for a week to look like you. This is unfair. *I'm* having a baby!" She rounds the table and crouches next to the stroller. Looking up at Tess, she covers her mouth with one hand. "Oh, she's absolutely beautiful."

Tess has always liked Amanda, who would often include her in group situations, pulling her into a debate and offering Tess up as an expert on something she barely knew anything about. It was all at once fun and frightening.

"Thank you." Tess tilts her head and smiles.

"So, this is Emilia! Love the name too!" She reaches out to cup Tess's hand, and Tess closes her other hand over Amanda's. "Are you sure you won't bring her to the office?"

Tess shakes her head, her lips sealing into a tight thin line. "Not a good time for me right now to face everyone."

Amanda's expression falls but her beauty never diminishes. Just then, the waiter asks if they're ready to order drinks. Amanda asks for the house white, and Tess follows suit. Menus are left, but Amanda's stare is too engaging for Tess to ignore.

"Sam left me," she puts bluntly. Amanda pushes back from the table. "About a month ago."

"Tess." Her friend is speechless. Her impossibly large eyes grow larger as her hands reach to cover her mouth.

"It's okay," Tess tries to reassure her, shaking her head. "I'm okay; Emma's okay." She reaches into the stroller and pulls the blanket level with her sleeping daughter's bare neck. Tess had made up her mind that she would share this information with Amanda, saving her the painful and repetitive discussions when she went back to work in a few months, knowing her friend would relay the information systematically.

Over lunch, Tess shares most of what she knows about what happened and why. They break to eat quiche and sip their wine, but her sad news dominates the lunch.

"You know, I have a friend who just went through something like this, and he went to a counselor and swore it saved his life." Amanda waves the server over and asks that her wine be refilled. Tess nods to another glass when asked and considers her friend's suggestion.

Looking past Amanda, Tess's eyes are drawn to the hospital that sits atop the hill bordering the city's southwest end. "I hear the hospital has a new wing dedicated to psychiatry. It's one of those places that design programs around a person's specific needs."

Amanda follows her stare and then looks back in surprise. "You're not *crazy*; you don't need to go to a *hospital.* Just look into a counselor; they're a dime a dozen."

Tess smiles and nods, never taking her eyes from the hilltop. "Yeah, it costs like eight hundred dollars a day, but my insurance would pay a portion if my doctor signed off on the stay." Tess finds comfort in the architecture of the building, and the idea that she could stay there for a time intrigues her.

"That's a LOT of money! Just consider counseling." Amanda cleans the lipstick from the rim of her glass. "It's one of those things that play on your mind - you guys were together a long time."

Tess listens with a blank stare, watching Amanda's lips form word after word. She could never understand how anybody could talk so much about anything. Even in her career, Tess only spoke when absolutely necessary to get a point across or give direction. She nods as Amanda continues, undeterred, about how she ought to deal with this challenging time in her life.

As Amanda gets up to return to work, Tess decides that therapy is the way to approach the emotions she's been suffering of late and tells her friend that she will get help.

"It couldn't hurt."

BUY HER PAST'S PRESENT

Other Books of Fiction by Michael Poeltl

1. The Judas Syndrome
2. Rebirth (Book 2 of The Judas Syndrome)
3. Revelation (Book 3 of The Judas Syndrome)
4. Her Past's Present
5. Waning Metaphorically (14 Short Stories)
6. A.I. Insurrection – The General's War
7. A.I. Insurrection – Armageddon (Book 2 of the A.I. Series)
8. A.I. Insurrection – Exodus (Book 3 of the A.I. Series)
9. The Blind Affect

Young Reader Picture Books

1. West of Noreso
2. An Angry Earth

Educational Books by Michael Poeltl

1. If a Tree Falls in the Forest...
2. Energy is Forever, and so are YOU!

About the author

Author Website: www.mikepoeltl.com

Amazon Author Page: Michael Poeltl Amazon

Facebook Page: Michael.Poeltl.Author

Goodreads Author Page: Goodreads

Twitter Handle: @mpoeltlauthor

Instagram: mpoeltl.author

Further Acknowledgements

To whomever, or whatever is seeding my brain with these tales, narratives, and oddities: Gratitude.

Reviews and requests for interviews and guest blogs are always appreciated!

www.ingramcontent.com/pod-product-compliance
Lightning Source LLC
Chambersburg PA
CBHW020418260626
47156CB00007B/2453